No More Heroes

J R Endeacott

Relish Books

First published in 2005 by Relish Books, Leeds, UK.

www.relishbooks.co.uk

ISBN 0-9547-844-2-1

Cover Design: Chris Archer.

General Editing: Jackie Beedle, Jane Selby.

Distributed by Gardners Books, Eastbourne, and Relish Books, Leeds.

A Catalogue for this book is available from the British Library.

Printed and bound by Clifford Press Ltd., Coventry.

RELISH NUMBER 3

Dedicated to

Kathryn, Helen & Sue.

1   Long and Winding Roads

'Let's play a game' a voice suggested.

We were on the bleak coach trek back from the Portsmouth-Leeds game one bleak Saturday night in the bleak early 1980's.

Seven or eight men agreed - some I didn't even know yet had travelled great distances with - and the idea was encouraged and cultivated.

'Call it The Alphabet Game,' came the voice again, then he told us the rules; they weren't exactly hard to follow.

Such distractions were crucial for long journeys back from Leeds' Division Two away games, the boredom could be excruciating. Expense *was* spared on the quality of the transport in which we endured thousands of boring, bumcheek-numbing miles. Very occasionally you'd get a TV on the coach. And very, *very* occasionally it would actually work properly. Videos were way too much of a luxury then for such proceedings. Even the radio was virtually always broken and don't even think about there being a toilet on board, we're talking prehistoric times. That meant you couldn't even drink yourself stupid unless you were willing to risk wetting yourself or humiliating yourself by *spillingly* peeing into a communal (and warm and slippery) plastic bottle.

The objective of the first ever game of Alphabet had been to name bands with each letter of the alphabet and if you took longer than ten seconds to name one, you were out. All pretty humdrum fun but it passed the time away. Shame we never played for money with that particular version, I was an aspiring know-all in rock and pop. I was good at making them up too, just in case. This next, more difficult version all sort of got out of hand and the rules seemed to distort and bend beyond recognition the longer the game went on. Something along the lines of...

'Alphabet - Illnesses and Ailments.   Steve, you start, with A,' instructed Banksy, and so I did.

'*Arthritis.*'

'*Bronchitis,*' then said Mike; and so it went on as others joined in.

'*Cholera.*'

'*Diarrhoea.*'

'*Earache.*'

'*Objection!*'

'*Overruled. Next, F,*' said referee Banksy.

'*Frostbite.*'

'*Gout.*'

'*Herpes.*'

'*Influenza.*'

'*Er... jelly-botty.*'

'*You're out, on your way, laddie.*'

'*Jimmy Adamson?*'

'*And you, and that's not funny at any rate.*'

'*Jaundice.*'

'*Kleptomania.*'

'*Dodgy, but...*'

'*Leprosy.*'

'*Measles.*'

'*Neuralgia.*'

'*Old age.*'

'*Nope, send him down!*'

'*That's prejudice is that.*'

'*No it's not, I just don't like you.*'

'*Well that's fair enough, you should've said so.*'

'*Er... osteoporosis.*'

'*Pleurisy.*'

'*Queerness.*'

'*Yeah right. You're out. I mean you're disqualified.*'

'*Quinsy.*'

'*What, Jack Klugman's an illness?*'

'*It looks like it hurts him every time he smiles, that's true enough.*'

'*Rheumatism.*'

'*Syphilis.*'

'*Tonsillitis.*'

'*Ugliness?*'

'*Upset stomach?*'

'*Urethritis.*'

'*Varicose veins.*'
'*Writer's cramp?*'
'*Wind?*'
'*No, out.*'
'*But you let him have 'ugliness'!*'
'*It's an 'ard life, old son.*'
'*Warts?*'
'*That's acceptable.*'
'*X breathing?*'
'*Eczema?*'
'*Xenophobia!*'
'*Yellow Fever.*'
Then a pregnant pause, gestation period of about a minute.
'*Z anyone?*'
'*Zowie Bowie?*'
'*Zip-caught tail?*'
'*Ouch!*'
'*Sleeping sickness.*'
'*That'll do. Back to A.*'
'*Deafness.*'
'*Eh? Oh, good one.*'
'*Alzheimer's.*'
'*Bee sting. Bad cold...*'
'*Birth?*'
'*Crabs? C-sickness?*'
'*Coitus interruptus.*'
'*Get real.*'
'*It's plagued me, I've not had a jump for years.*'
'*Blimey, I wonder why.*'
'*Denial.*'
'*No.*'
'*I refuse to accept that.*'
'*Refuse all you like; it's a river anyway.*'
'*Death.*'
'*Emorrhoids.*'
'*Ead cold, eadache?*'
'*Flatulence. Oops, excuse me.*'
'*Aaargh, you smelly-arsed swine!*'
'*I know - 'king Tourettes.*'

7

'Two what?'
'It's a mental illness.'
'Hangover.'
'So's that an' all.'
'Homosexuality.'
'Homophobia.'
'Itchy feet? Insanity!'
'I don't feel too good!'
'Jug earedness.'
'Knock kneedness.'
'Knob rot.'
'Life.'
'Limp wristed.'
'Lumps.'
'Marriage.'
'My head hurts.'
'Mum, I don't feel well!'
'Nosebleed.'
'Nearly dead.'
'Odd looking.'
'Off sick.'
'Period pains.'
'It's just a myth.'
'Piles.'
'Q anyone?'
'Queuing, that's a British disease.'
'Quite poorly.'
'QPR's offside trap; makes me ill any road.'
'Alzheimer's!'
'Runs.'
'Really bad cold.'
'Royal Family.'
'Red!'
'Saturday Night Fever.'
'Sex.'
'The clap.'
'Thick head.'
'Thick ear?'
'TB.'

'*Trots.*'
'*Anyone got a U?*'
'*U look terrible mate.*'
'*Under the weather.*'
'*Under fed.*'
'*Under Milkwood.*'
'*Unplanned pregnancy?*'
'*You should know!*'
'*VD.*'
'*So should you!*'
'*Virginity.*'
'*Walking funny.*'
'*Wedding vows.*'
'*Well ill.*'
'*Wan...*'
'*Steady, there's women on board!*'
'*That's a good one - 'women' as an illness.*'
'*I can sense some bitterness tonight.*'
'*Wooden leg. How about that?*'
'*Ex wife, talking of bitter.*'
'*Express Newspapers - Mancs after all...*'
'*Young Conservatives.*'
'*Are we home yet?*'

* * *

2   Indelible

1980's life was a dog, and I was a pig. Teenagers shouldn't have to worry about stuff, they should enjoy life as one big, responsibility-free party. But me, eldest spawn of Mrs and the late Mr Jim Bottomley, I had problems in life aplenty. Pretty much the same as any other poor sap, true, but you don't worry about what gruel life's serving others when you've got bowlfuls of your own. For much of the time my main problem was Leeds United, they were really depressing, their plight darkened days and haunted nights. Supporting them could be and often was a right bitch. Many of us spent more time and money than was decent watching the team, desperate for a return to the glory years of the '60s and '70s. It wasn't happening and in 1982, Leeds were rubbish and were relegated. They deserved it. I wanted to rid the whole rotten season from my system but it wasn't always such an easy thing to do.

Drinking, carrying on and just being out with the lads helped, for a few hours each week anyway. Beer was my friend and socialising was my fix. I lived for the weekend, I couldn't wait for each next one. You don't fret about hangovers when you're enjoying creating them. Well I didn't anyway; at least, not then. I loved getting drunk, letting the feeling of pleasant, amusing delirium flood my senses while my inhibitions lowered and my self confidence peaked. Whilst inebriated you know 'exactly' what you're doing, convinced too that you're carrying it out all very well. Being reminded the next day of your exploits makes for captivating listening - much of it simply could not have happened, you could not have been such a pillock. It certainly *had* happened but the awareness, along with the drink and particles of grey matter, had been squirted plentifully against various porcelain walls.

About football: in Leeds we'd suffered the decline of the country's once greatest club, since 1975 when we were cheated out of the European Cup. The rot set in proper from that miserable Paris night. Paris, the City of Romance? Get stuffed, it was rancid and heart-breaking. Supporting Leeds, you needed to be resilient - everyone loved to abuse us - but we lost the resilience and just about caved in, especially on the pitch. After the defeat to Munich, other bad stuff happened, including great players leaving, for pitifully small transfer fees. For all the graft they'd put in helping make the club great, they were sold and treated cheaply by the Board, as if they wanted to get rid of them as quickly as possible. There were still great players there but after Don Revie, losing Billy Bremner, Johnny Giles, Norman Hunter and co wrenched the real heart from the club.

'80s days were when, as a young man, it really mattered what you wore and what music you liked. Fila, Tacchini, Lacoste, Adidas, Burberry, Pringle, and so on, sport and leisure wear was vital for your street cred. Also, you were 'out' in the cool stakes if you didn't conform musically. Course, I couldn't give a toss, about what clothes and music I was supposed to favour, I listened to and wore what I liked. Mind you, I had my hair cut like Bernard Sumner's - it's a good job I wasn't blond else I'd have looked like Hitler bleeding Youth. And I never wore flares for strides, **never**, I didn't want to be that different and I wasn't mentally deranged. All the trendy football 'casuals' stole their gear or at least got it knocked off. Robbing was wrong, I'd learned that to my pain. Not that I resented anyone for wearing stolen gear, it was their choice, nothing to do with me. Anyway, to be fair(ish), shoplifting was better than mugging people, which has always been the behaviour of the lowest lowlife scum, simple as that.

Regards clothing tastes, for my feet I did insist on quality clobber. For work and for supping I insisted on wearing Dr Marten shoes or proper well-made brogues. Doc Marts were always the business, genuinely great British workmanship. They were absolute animals to break in though, with blisters on my heel and blood in the soles of my shoes genuinely not uncommon. The agony was eventually worth it as the shoes softened to become trusty and well-tamed loyal servants. Someone once told me that if you looked after your feet, your feet would look after you. It might seem a daft old wives' tale I know (a bit harsh on old wives if you ask me) but it was always relevant whenever I shopped for treads. Actually, in the not too-distant past, it had been shop*lifting*, with trainers at any rate. I'd raided Lillywhite's on more than a few occasions, always picking Adidas Bamba or Sambas. I was a discerning thief you see; and I had good taste. It wasn't so many pairs to be fair and a conscience eventually did grow in me. I decided finally to *buy* all my trainers - at Lillywhite's - as a little gesture of apology sort of. And their prices weren't exactly low, mark my words, no wonder people nicked from them.

I did care about what I wore really, it was just I was too tight to pay over-the-odds prices for tissue thin tracksuits and the like which would last about as long as a Leeds clean sheet. And unfortunately, I'd had to bin my bright blue Harrington jacket because circles of sweat like Saturn's Rings had started to stain the armpits. They'd begun to hum a bit too just to add to the aura. I loved that jacket an' all - like Linus and his towel - and I hardly had it off my back. That might explain the perspiration, thinking about it. That along with my school days fear of talking to girls, specifically my Top Five Totty League.

To replace the Harrington I strangely took a fancy to a Crombie overcoat advertised in the NME by Christopher Robin Clothing. It was identical (in their picture at least) to those that Madness wore, complete with red silk lining. I wasn't even much of a ska fan but I just knew I'd look immaculate in a Crombie, I was convinced of it. It cost twenty-five notes and I 'had to wait a long three months for the experience. The wait for delivery depressed me to Eeyore pro-portions, I tell you. When it finally did arrive I tried it on and hated it straight away; I looked a right prannock. I sent it back and ended up getting another Harrington, black this time to suit my mood and my self-worth, from Class on Lower Briggate. It was an achieve-ment managing to actually reach the Class boutique with the seven quid intact as I had to pass the Starlight Amusements to get there. It took another six months for my refund for the Crombie to arrive, and then it came from the NME - the clothing company had gone bust. Cor blimey, it served them right, blinking Londoners. I sent the NME a poem to thank them, thinking what a nice and decent thing it was to do. What a nice lad I thought I was until my customary teenage disdain took over and I realised what a noodle I was. Still, not a noodle in an odd looking, ill-fitting Crombie.

* * *

When I was thirteen, I tried killing myself. Not over Leeds United but over a girl. She never found out, fortunately. She never will either. I didn't like poison, it made me sick, and - as you can tell - the suicide attempt failed and I didn't not live to regret it. Thankfully. As a result though, I had a retching laburnum seed hangover for days and a face paler than Billy Bremner's kneecaps. *Plus* a strange new sensation, like a scar on the vision after staring at a brightness too long. Every time I awoke I had a tune with me, every day for the rest of my life. It sounds dubious I know but it's true. A song, always a different one, accompanied me, on every single new day. The first morning after the night of green and black laburnum seeds, me retching more vomit than a vomit making factory on overtime, had *Your Mother Should Know* by The Beatles haunting my return to living. My dreams had been weird - not so surprising really, with poison chundering away inside me - consisting mostly of the Super Leeds team winning the FA Cup at Wembley. Oh, not forgetting me, John, Paul, George and Ringo in the team too incidentally, and doing a lap of honour round the Wembley pitch. Ringo I remember was particularly giddy. I always preferred him, he was easily the best Beatle in my book. From all that I surmised - *naturally* you could say - that the Leeds players and The Beatles saved my life. Yes, I'm aware some folk would say what an unbelievable, incredible dream it was, and I admit it, I really couldn't disagree with them. I mean, Leeds United winning the FA Cup again, *get a grip!*

To be dead straight about it, I was never exactly proud about trying to kill myself. Fortunately no one ever found out then. *Now,* it's hardly relevant; I had been a prick. My Dad died not knowing about it, which was sort of good - I'd have been even more screwed up if it had been his final memory of me. Jesus, the time after his death was all desperate. Minutes felt like weeks, days like months. I don't know how my Mum coped, never mind me or my younger brother Andrew. If I'd have thought about the guilt and misery they'd have suffered, I'd have gone nowhere near suicide.

* * *

With my Dad being an avid and loyal Leeds supporter, I reckon my Mum handled it right. She didn't see Leeds United as competition or as his mistress but just his main innocent distraction. Even though she probably wouldn't admit it and hardly ever went to a game, she loved Leeds too in her own way. She actually insisted I carried on supporting them after my Dad, even if my doing so no doubt hurt her: I looked like my Dad as well as acted like him apparently; I even sounded like him. That must have been really eerie. In truth I never had plans to stop supporting them, the family allegiance would never stop and if I ever spawned kids it would continue exactly that way. We never got on that well, me and my Mum, but it was good we could agree on certain things every now and then. Following a football team has always been more than just a pastime, it's a relationship, a *faith,* and it feels good knowing you're not alone in the same cause. It's almost like family in fact. The Great Leeds United players had been like family - our brothers and our uncles - and when they played well, it felt like they were doing it for all of us.

Like football teams *should*, music had the power to inspire. Those songs in my head every morning were there for a reason, a good reason, even if they got annoying. Whichever one woke me, it tattooed my mind and even occasionally became an omen for the coming day. I told a couple of school-friends about it, how special this mysterious occurrence felt and how I just knew it was for a reason. They thought I'd lost my mind.

3   Rolling Stoned

Good job the summer of 1982 was warm because we were still shivering from the bitter chill of Leeds' relegation in May. Time is a great healer though, especially summer time. Yep, it was a proper summer, with at least two weeks of warm, even hot, sunshine, vast improvement on your usual damp and goose-pimply British cold-waves. So pleasant and dry in fact, that the region's slugs will have been grossly unhappy. *This seemingly pointless remark bears more meaning later.*

Me, Mark, Bruges, Rick and Dave had all freely bought into the prospect of a Sunday afternoon in the sunshine at a concert publicised all over the shop. Although it meant the cancellation of our customary Sunday football match on Cross Flatts Park, we all felt such sacrifices had to be made every now and then. Besides, football, due to United's misfortunes, had lost much of its magic locally, with clouds of depression still in existence over the parks and pitches. The faith and enthusiasm would return, football fandom never totally leaves the Northern soul, it just needs a sabbatical every now and then. Anyhow, in the summer, music and girls were more important pastimes and in this gig an exciting prospect was coming our way. Away from us five, I couldn't understand how the other lads on our scene weren't as interested in the concert. It was a big event for the city after all, not just in a musical sense. Still, it was their choice, their regret.

What a brilliant year '82 was for concerts in Leeds. I took our Andrew to see Queen at Elland Road and they were bloody great. There was a bit of trouble at the gig too; always adding to the fun, for me anyway. Watching trouble that is, not actually being a part of it. Rock fans were bottling and canning The Teardrop Explodes - who actually were very good and not deserving of such crap - and more than a few fans near the stage ended up bloodied and concussed.

15

The Rolling Stones were bigger than Queen in those days, even though I think the 'power' switched position over the years. We weren't exactly great fans of the Stones, any of us, and we didn't have tickets and weren't willing to pay for any either, it was just that we weren't intending missing out on the whole occasion. Even if we'd fail to actually see anyone perform we'd be able to hear them, away from the arena, that was for sure.

The plan was for us to at least sit, soak and drink in the good atmosphere and - you never know - maybe even pull. We'd take in a few rays near the perimeters of the concert, swig our vodka and get legless. With respect to the band, rather than being a fan I couldn't take to Mick Jagger's singing, his sharp voice bugged me, simple as that. Not on every song fair enough but on enough of them to matter. You wouldn't hear me denying they had some great tunes and that Keith Richards was a cock-on guitarist but I just couldn't take to the overall Stones sound. True, I was always well biased in favour of The Beatles, having listened to the Fab Four since my very early days. Also, not that it mattered so much to a lad, it has to be said that Mick and the boys were well ugly. They could crack a cracked mirror, bless them. At least The Beatles didn't put you off your food. Or your water. Or your sleep even. I didn't exactly see myself as an oil painting - unless Picasso had a *Rough* Period - but these guys took the (dog) biscuit and 1940's midwives deserved danger money, for the peril of turning to stone whilst delivering such cuties. Nevertheless, they were true superstars (the Stones, not the midwives), the biggest on the world stage of music, and they were flying to humble old Leeds and its stunningly attractive 60's architecture and pretty high-rise blocks of flats.

It was obvious though, something would go wrong, this was Leeds after all; the city was like the football team: once great, majestic, unpredictable, even unlucky, now in certain ways, on its knees. For one thing, despite the forecasts we expected showers of rain by the bucket load. The last time I'd been to Roundhay Park was with my Dad a few years before he died. To see The Wombles. Yes, The Wombles, in person. Well no, The Wombles in ... womble. They *weren't* men (or women for that matter) dressed in furry costumes at all, they *were* The Wombles, believe it. I loved them and hurtled from school every time so as not to miss their show. But even I realised wombles couldn't swim and that day it absolutely pelted it down, thunder and lightning, the lot. The deeper and deeper the rainfall got the higher my disappointment became.

* * *

We'd arranged to meet at The Blooming Rose at lunch opening time. It's in Hunslet though never felt like anything but Beeston to me; strange that. There is something exciting and gloriously manly about being the first customers in a pub, knocking the doors down - like we were, figuratively speaking - even on a Sunday. Eventually, most of our Sundays would revolve around the *official* footie team Cross Flatts XI, which we would soon form from the motley crew of lads who gathered in Cross Flatts Park to take on all comers. That's another story. We were all just about baptised on beer in the Rose, due mainly to the famously good hand-pulled Tetley Bitter and the rarity of scrapping and bother there. In the tap room usually was a smashing bloke with a mass of silvery grey hair, in his forties, called Den Fearnville, and he used to go on about the scores of people queuing to get in for their fix of the renowned brew. He was a good, entertaining source of info on just about anything going, including old Leeds games and the former players.

At the Rose they still pulled a great pint and it was cheap (always a sweetener) as was the video game in the tappie, which I frequently took advantage of, to the annoyance of less skilled, non-gaming mates. 10p to play, it was my all time favourite game: *Mr Do*. And - though at the risk of sounding big headed - I was by far the best player in the pub. Not surprising really, I'd undergone hours and hours and hours of intensive, expensive training in town on Mill Hill. It was actually named *Mr Do!* complete with the exclamation mark which gave it a sillier moniker and threatened to trivialise what was in virtual reality, an absolute classic. In terms of gaming, it was a bit like Pac Man, though better, with a little fella who looked like Noddy (and thus an old mate of mine) gathering cherries up for points while being chased by monsters. He had a magic ball that he (*you*) threw at them to kill them - until the next stage - and he could also crush them to death by pushing apples on them to earn you more points. And you'd get extra points for collecting the different pieces of food and a free game and eight thousand points if you could grab the mega rare diamond when it flashed on the screen with a high pitched siren. And not forgetting the chance of an extra life by collecting the E, X, T, R and A icons. It had its own tune too, a bit like Disneyland's *'It's a Small World'* only daintier and even more bloody annoying.

Chess *Mr Do!* wasn't but it was an all-time great and deserves right on respect above even *Space Invaders*, *Galaxian*, *PacMan*, *Kill Hitler*, *Snap the Judge*, *Explode the Pimp* and *Dump on the Gnu*. I made those last four up, you might've guessed.

Alas, going to the Mill Hill slots finally became too much for me. I'd never really enjoyed entering the amusement arcade den in the daytime and leaving at night as it was, but coming out of there with the bonus of bleary eyes, shakes and cold-sweats got too much. Often I got to not sleep at night for thinking of the carnage and destruction I could inflict in that fantastic world of kaleidoscopic video conflict, and the number of lives (and coins) I wasted there really was disgraceful. *And* I lost count of the dreams I had, of the ropey blonde cashier dragging me away from the video games and pinball machines to the back room, where she'd rip down my trousers and seduce me greedily. She never did in reality and it was her loss, my flesh strategies and manoeuvres were legendary. Well, on my own planet at least.

* * *

After a few pints, we nipped into a nearby offie for 'proper' booze and caught the bus on Dewsbury Road to take us all the way up to Roundhay Park. It was half full already and would soon be crammed with passengers via town for the concert. We were in high spirits, it was all exciting, thousands of people from all over the country, world even, heading for the same place as ourselves and all in equally good spirits. The only possible way I could have felt more thrilled would have been for such a gig to be held at our Cross Flatts Park, unlikely as that was.

On the top deck the five of us were performing the old orange juice ploy. There was no way we'd be allowed to be seen in public getting drunker and drunkerer on vodka, we'd be collared for D&D straight away, so we poured most of the bottled orange out of the back window and mixed in the vodka. We sensibly refrained from immediately guzzling the vodka and orange as we knew it would make us paralytic much too quickly to be real fun. If ever there was a person who enjoyed causing a bit of trouble amongst the lads however, it was Rick; and so we were sensible for approximately two minutes before he took a big swig. Thus there was a near white riot as the rest of us fcared we wouldn't get any. Well, a *four-man* white riot and a *one-man* black riot, to be more accurate, as Mark was black. He still is actually, as far as I'm aware. I could never really decide whether it needed mentioning or not, to be honest. There it is then, mentioned, and my indecision decisively is desisted. I feel okay about it too, I'll sleep easy.

Talking of not getting any, Dave frequently was - not getting any and frequently talking about it - and he felt the need to keep reminding us that he hadn't had sex for ninety-nine consecutive days. We all tried to avoid physical contact with him, especially in crowded areas, just to be on the safe side. As to why he felt such need to share was beyond me and the fact that he had gave me the attitude of *Long may it continue* just to be mischievous. Counting the days of not having sex, how bad, how blooming sad, was that? I'd never counted, primarily because I had nothing to count as I was still a virgin.

We jumped off the bus about a mile away from Roundhay Park at a crowded junction. The traffic was heavy and the bus was struggling to complete its route or even wedge into the long lane of cars. There were hundreds of pedestrians too, milling about all over the place. The bus driver was not a happy man, and our thanking him brightly probably added to his state of not-a-happy-man-ness. Our slow walk very quickly became a drag, with traffic crawling by us, though not the bus obviously, and alcohol and sunshine made my feet ache more. One vehicle, a small beige and white VW camper van with a longhaired woman in the front passenger seat, arm resting on the open window, passed us. She had a flowered headband on and a flowered man sitting next to her. There was a joke in there somewhere - flowers and camper - but I refrained out of politeness and respect, and alcoholic apathy. The duo just had to be '60's children'. Mark and Rick jogged up to ask for a lift. Pleasantly surprised, the occupants said a cheerful yes (two cheerful yes'es) telling us to hop in the back. We stooped in, nearly as difficult as hopping as you can imagine. They were in their late thirties I guessed and were great folk. We offered them vodka, they offered us egg mayonnaise and cress sandwiches, of which there seemed to be dozens. We accepted more food than they did drink, no doubt about that.

We'd grown up in aggressive times with regard to music, where it seemed you *had* to be a fan of one kind and no other, and any fans of 'opposing' styles were scorned and ridiculed, even set on. It probably began with the alleged mods versus rockers fighting, or the teddy boys against anyone who didn't want to look as stupid, but *we* never had the same attitude. What would have been the point? I think that's what I most liked about these mates, that you could 'be' just about whatever, *who*ever you wanted, with little criticism for it. It felt cool being that way, very cool. At High School, whatever your opinion on subjects like music, films, footballers, actresses even, it would be challenged and sneered at by loads of the others. And if your opinion wasn't popular then very possibly neither were you. I was never ever any cop at accepting criticism, specially physical. In fact, being on the receiving end of verbal and physical stick scared me; it made me sick with fear. It was a near constant battle to conceal my real feelings if ever I was insulted. I'd try to grin and bear whatever ridicule was aimed at me, and I think I did a decent job of it, but I was boiling inside, I hated the sarcasm and mockery always lurking in the background as if it was on the bloody syllabus. And that even included from a few of the teachers.

We cascaded out of the camper van and thanked the two hippies, as I suppose they could be called. I've no idea what their names were but their lack of misgivings at four slightly inebriated lads and one more inebriated lad (Mark never could take his drink) piling in to the back of their van was fab. And even with my home-made Stranglers 'Ugly' t-shirt (of Karloff's Frankenstein monster) and a couple of Clash ones on the others, they didn't seem to care one bit, they were nothing but charming and friendly. *That's* what music and concerts should do, unite people of different status or background, get them celebrating, partying, and not falling out.

The 'earth' arena of Roundhay Park never possessed much by way of perimeter fencing or walls of any real note in the first place, so the organizers had to erect stretches of huge ten by ten foot wooden boards and nail them together. It was strangely impressive in a Steve McQueen *Great Escape* kind of way. It was sort of offensive at the same time too though: how dare they invade our park to put up fences to stop the people getting in? There were no apparent protests at this hometown exclusion but I wager I wasn't the only one aggrieved. It doesn't take much to rile Leeds folk in general, let's be honest, but those huge fences were not built just to stop non-payers attending a gig, they were there to oppress the proles of our city. *Heed my words, Comrades!* Okay, we weren't in Berlin and we weren't Pink Floyd, but this damned wall was out of order. Feats of modern engineering anyway, the fences weren't, even Donald Pleasance would've seen that; he might even have fancied his chances of climbing them.

Walking around the park outside the acres of bordering barriers was fun. There were thousands of people just sitting on the grass spending a cosy afternoon picnicking in warm sunshine. Groups of lads walked around; groups of white lads, groups of black lads and (even) groups of Asian lads, and looking for nothing but fun. In fact, banter was exchanged between them and the officers of the law, to the extent of even sharing drinks and ice cream. And whenever the DJ spoke to the audience on the other side (the fence, not Earthly Life) the cheers and applause were hugely uplifting. Never mind half the population of Leeds, it sounded like half the country was inside, much louder than a Leeds United sell out and louder even than when 48,000 people were at Elland Road in 1977 for the Queen's Silver Jubilee.

There was a gap under one of the hoardings, we were the first to spot it. Caused by the dip in the ground directly beneath, we couldn't quite believe no one else had investigated, in the way a budding Boycott would inspect a wicket and crease. And there were no police or security positioned outside there to monitor the area so something must be up, something we hadn't noticed. How come no one else had seen the opportunity, what were we missing? Alcohol always had the potential to inspire and we more than fancied our chances of squeezing through to the concert. But were we being too cocky then? Maybe, but sense prevailed, at least temporarily. The urge to dive under the barrier was near overwhelming but we had to ignore it and instead flopped down on to the springy turf a few yards away to consider our options. Officers on duty did appear every now and then, casually patrolling the acres of green, taking nice, relaxing strolls in the park on a pleasant over time Sunday afternoon. Our overcoming-by-going-under this obstacle would be like playing *Frogger*, our avoiding being squashed trying to cross a busy road like the frog in the video game. And assuming we achieved our aim, what was waiting for us at the other side? I'd heard the Stones used their own particular and very tough *security force* for concerts.

The reputation of Hell's Angels bikers preceded them (as you might have just noticed) even if sometimes their physical presence never actually appeared where those reputations did. They were maniacs, notorious for kicking at least ten bells out of people and asking questions later, even murdering rival sect members and operating above the law as untouchables in all sorts of rackets. They were worse than the Met, the West Midlands police and even some of the less discerning club doormen of Leeds, who all thought they ruled the world with their crooked ways. The Rolling Stones had always had many Angels followers and it turned out some were on duty today as security and bouncers. Dozens were strutting around - not that I dared scrutinise them too closely - and I'd never seen so much facial hair, so many denims and leathers, chains and tattoos in all my life. And God knows what the men looked like.

The worry of getting nicked was bad enough, the threat of being beaten to a pulp by meathead bikers was even more frightening. My heart increased its rate of percussion - Charlie Watts would have been impressed - as we whispered of our chances. Preparation was everything, my Mum always said; well, take a skeg at this for preparation: -

\#   Drinking far too much vodka;

\#   Discussing far too little our options;

\#   Not actually deciding on a plan in the end anyway.

But not to worry, we'd be okay as long as we were calm and collected, and as long as we definitely didn't do anything too impuls...
'Ricky, you stupid bastard!' Mark cried as Rick shot up and ran towards the fence to breach it. It was stupid, but stupidly impressive too. Stupid-er still though, we were right behind him almost straight away (he was never the quickest of lads).

We were like sheep with lemming leanings. Waiting for him to slip under the fence was more intense than queuing for the bog with your bladder straining and your kidneys crying for mercy. It was madness (no it wasn't, it was the Stones hey hey) we were like over excited school kids lining up to escape into... well, God knows what. *Our* side of the fence was safety, the other was an exhilarating danger zone. This is when the vodka was priceless encouragement, together with the increasing calls of '*Go on, lads!*' and '*Good on you, son!*' from more than a few spectators. Rick, though the tallest, was agile and accustomed to diving about, being a half-decent goalkeeper and over-drinking rugby playing student and so it took him just an instant to hit the ground and slide through the gap. I was last in line: I hated that, being last, but I had little choice as I was naturally the quietest and least pushy of the five. Mark went next, and he was nippier than a nippy-type person, then Bruges, who also seemed to not-mind-the-gap with ease. Come my turn, and I suddenly see the gap shrink. I'm too big for it, I'll end up like Winnie the Pooh after honey! I couldn't turn back now, imagine the shame.

I threw myself to the ground (being hammered, it wasn't difficult - the ground might have actually jumped up at me) and positioned my head sideways to slot under the hoarding. I brought my arms around to pull myself through to the other side and then felt myself grabbed under the armpits, dragged through and hauled upwards. Painlessly I scuffed my lower back and arse on the wood. Rick was pulling me through; I'd never been so pleased to see him in all my days. Dizzy and light headed, I realised we were in another world.

He snapped me to my senses with '*Run like the bollocks, in to the crowd!*' pointing down the hill to a huge construction covered in black tarpaulin, with throngs of people gathered and milling around the front of it. I wasn't totally sure how to run like the bollocks - surely it'd be 'roll' - but I think I got his drift. We were standing at the top of a big grass slope almost horizontal to the stage a hundred or so yards away. From where I was looking down, to our left were thousands of people sitting on the grass terrace. I saw Bruges bounding down the hill, arms aloft like the great Peter Lorimer, with Mark waiting for him at the bottom (Bruges not Lorimer, I'm not sure whether or not Hot Shot was hot on the Stones). I bolted after him. There were no foaming-at-the-mouth Angels or tetchy coppers chasing us with weapons, instead there were just people shouting at us.

Running and bounding like a drunken sheep junior I assumed they were jeering me so I started to flick V-signs all around. Then I realised they were *supporting* me, I was a rebel and a have-a-go hero and they were cheering and laughing - *for* me, *for ME!* It was fantastic. I flew down that bumpy home straight of a hill and ran in to Mark and Bruges - literally - at the foot of the incline, I almost hugged them I was so elated. We were on the edge of a large human sea, eager to dive in as the DJ tried to whip up enthusiasm for the first act appearing, Joe Jackson. Except we three should have been five, and no way could we enjoy the gig until we were all there, present and (in)correct.

4 Under the Influence

SENSATIONALIST HEADLINE WRITERS SHOULD BE GIVEN LONG SENTENCES!!!

Proud of that one I was. I made it up while reading of the 'chaos and carnage' which had beset the city of Leeds at the Stones gig - not reportedly or allegedly but *definitely* and *fact* according to the papers.

They said thousands had rioted and wrought havoc at Roundhay Park, with scores of arrests for violent disorder, illegal entry and similar stuff. Exactly what really happened is a bit vague, especially to drunks like me and the lads for instance, and to those not actually there like most of the reporters for instance. But the *'Never let fact get in the way of a good story'* sort of rubbish was well wrong for the UK. The truth, proudly speaking from my hazy point of view, was that we'd been rebels, scamming our way in to an expensive concert for free. It wasn't a punk thing, it was possibly just symptomatic of Leeds people, taking no crap from no one. It was all exhilarating, all a smart buzz. Had we foreseen though that the section of the ten-foot barricade we'd slipped under would later be stormed, battered and broken by scores more, we might not have felt as proud.

'Where's Dave?' Rick was asked as he sauntered down the hill to join us.
'Don't ask me, the tart never came through.'
We didn't blame Rick. He wouldn't have cared if we had have.
'He was right behind you, wasn't he Steve?'
'Yeah I think so' I answered. I honestly couldn't remember, even though it had only been ten minutes prior. The vodka was playing mischief with the thing in my head meant to remember things. Sod it, if Dave wasn't right behind me then it was all his own fault, not mine. Then it struck me - in slow motion given the liquid-ness my head was paddling in - that Dave had our third and final vodka (and orange) bottle. All the time I'd known him, he'd had this reputation

for being untrustworthy and tight. He wouldn't sell his grandmother, he'd rent her out. It didn't take a Hitchcockian mind to calculate that he'd hung back deliberately so as to rip us off and keep the vodka to himself, or sell it even.

The DJ's final record was coming to a close (it could have been Rainbow's *Since You Been Gone*) and we had to decide whether to snake ourselves in to the crowd for Joe Jackson or go looking for Dave and the Smirnoff.

'Ah let's wait a bit for him, he might be looking for us,' Mark suggested. Not unreasonable an idea. After all, Dave was a big fan of Joe Jackson. And he had our drink (Dave that is, not Joe Jackson).

He wouldn't want to miss Joe Jackson performing, he'd really been looking forward to it.

And he had our drink.

Dave was a student at Portsmouth, where he said Joe Jackson had grown up so he felt they had a kind of connection.

And of course he had our drink, our last drink.

Joe Jackson was, despite being a fine pianist and a refined songwriter (and balding), a part of the new wave. He wrote about real life, working class youth, with lyrics about rejection, prejudice and unrequited love. *'Different for Girls'* and *'Is She Really Going Out with Him?'* were beauties - classics in fact, let's get it right - despite not doing that well in the charts. He was a street-wise, angry version of Elton John, only slimmer, more talented, more in touch with the real world, not ashamed of losing his hair and not a prima donna woolly woofter.

We waited a few more minutes at the foot of the hill. And there Dave was, he'd appeared, walking purposefully down the hill - without our bottle of vodka.

'I left it behind so went back for it but a copper spotted me,' he explained, with no sign of sorry.

'You lying thieving bastard!' came the chorus of disgust. He'd drunk it, or more likely, flogged it, as I think I'd mentally accused him of before. But then he put his arms out and shrugged as if to say *'What could I do?'* with a very weak effort to conceal a grin. *'Yeah you're right,'* he admitted, and pulled out the well-concealed full bottle from behind him. He'd McGuffinned us; or maybe it was just plain

McGuffed, I couldn't decide. Anyhow, he'd tricked us, the crafty beggar - *here's to him.*

The ease of how close to the stage we got proved how popular Joe Jackson wasn't.

The Rolling Stones had dozens of hit singles over the years the world over. My favourite was *(I Can't Get No) Satisfaction* with its fantastic guitar riff and classic line *'I can't get no girlie action'* which mirrored much of my teenage Beeston life, *too* much. I also really liked *Gimme Shelter* and *Paint It Black.* Others less so, like *Jumpin' Jack Flash, You Can't Always Get What You Want, Under My Thumb* and *Get Off Of My Cloud.* And then there's *Ruby Tuesday, Let's Spend the Night Together, Brown Sugar, Angie, Emotional Rescue* and, hoping desperately not to sound like one of those bloody awful K-Tel adverts, many, many more. No one could accuse them of being workshy, that was for sure, their output was massive, as was always Mick Jagger's energy, strutting and stretching, pouting and posing, and bouncing, blackguarding all over the earth's stages. All of those hits they'd created, all the great songs from that amazing repertoire: totally astounding. But whether they played any, all or none of them I was pretty much clueless, being that bollocksed from the booze.

The J Geils Band were the Stones' main support apparently, I was too drunk to know what they were like with absolutely no idea what they looked like even. Still, at least I didn't have to dwell on their two painful hit singles. Prior to them, Joe Jackson and his band I did remember; and they stole the show even though there wasn't really a show to steal from my puddled perspective.

* * *

On the warm Monday night, The Clash were playing Leeds Uni. I was still half-plastered when I got up. It was a Bank Holiday Monday as well. In Britain we're supposed to enjoy Bank Holidays but from my early drinking days I was always numb to them, having drunk far too much in the previous three days. It was usually a gloomy cloud of beer blues hanging over my dazed mind on those

Mondays more than anything else. It served me right I suppose, though paying to squirt your enjoyment against a wall and to wake up feeling miserable afterwards hardly seemed fair. In those maudlin times which were far too common for a young man to have to put up with, I wanted to be in the company of loved ones even if I was usually in dark mood. Preferably the company of a loving girlie in want of frequent *cuddling* but if womankind wasn't an option - which it was, all too often, not - then being with mates wasn't so bad an alternative.

The irony of us - like proper anarchists - nicking in to see the grandfathers of rock the day before and then paying to see punk godfathers The Clash the night after was too subtle to register. Probably due to the booze again, or youth. Worse that day, for me at least, was my being without a ticket, and this wasn't a concert you could steal in to.

Touts were charging a tenner for tickets officially priced at £3.50. In my league table of esteem, ticket touts were possibly as low as Man U fans, Tory MPs, Shakin Stevens, Michael Winner, fairies and Keith Chegwin, put together. And so I was sparring with my conscience about handing money over to the enemy of touts. Plus, to make me more split-opinionated - seriously, with no metropolitan racism involved - every single tout on the planet I ever met was a Scouser, or at least from near Merseyside.
An Economics joke (and how many of them can you say you've heard?): how do you set up the perpetual distribution of wealth in society? Put a crowd of Scousers in a room together.
Tealeaves and scallywags each and every one of them - *Got to pick a pocket or two!* No harsh stereotyping or generalisation of any sort there, obviously. I just couldn't bring myself to hand over my hard(ly) earned cash to them, it wasn't right, I had ethics, even if I kept them under guard much of the time. And then I saw Big Nath, about to start work at the entrance as a bouncer stroke ticket collector.

Big Nath Archer, from Headingley. In truth, not that big in reality, not from Headingley and maybe not even called Nath, but it's how I knew him. He and I had known each other at Matthew Murray though never as mates really, more like two of Ultravox's Passing Strangers, he was one of those kids who just got on with school life without much notice. He wasn't in any of my classes and he didn't play football so I hardly saw him. Now, he was a student and not only did he have a cool air about him, he looked like he could look after himself too, he'd broadened or 'filled out' as anyone who ever grows is described. He was in his second year of some degree at Leeds Poly, it might have been Chemistry, I forgot. His hair was long, daffy and curly - like that piano playing dog in the Muppets - and he looked, dare I say it, good.

Sort of renewing our sort of friendship one night, we'd challenged each other at pinball in The Skyrack in Headingley. I drank in Headingley a fair bit and sometimes would kip over on mates' settees and that. On the pinball the loser had to pay a fiver to the victor. It got quite dramatic - well, quite dramatic for the *Playboy* pinball, one of the slowest and dullest machines made - and I won the fifth, decisive game. In the Gents' bog he offered me a compromise - not that sort of compromise, we were never that close - consisting of a little polythene bag of cannabis plus a tiny piece of folded red paper. It was a 'wrap' containing a small amount of white powder. He convinced me the offer was much more fun and valuable than five quid and I believed him; it was hard not to, he had a persuasive manner. He'd've made a great salesman would Big Nath, he could sell knock off gear back to Liverpudlian scallies. What's more, he gave me an unofficial health warning about using substances. A salesman with a conscience, would you credit it. Weird, man.
'The cannabis will make you chilled, content,' he said. *'There's no known harm in it. The white stuff, that's 'speed' as it's mostly called. It'll launch you in to the sky, mate, I mean it.'* I listened quietly, impressed as if I was about to enter the stratosphere, privately excited at the prospect of new adventure. He carried on, *'But too much of it, too much using, has - like a foreskin, old pal - its drawbacks. You gotta be careful, it can harm you, just like alcohol. Not that a man of your intelligence should need telling, but I feel duty bound.'*
'Cheers Nath, appreciate it.' I didn't really, doing drugs was cool providing you weren't weak or stupid enough to go too far. I'd never be that weak or stupid, I was sure of it. He was needlessly delaying my trip to another weird and wonderful world, that's all. A

needleless weird and wonderful world too, better still; needles were bad, even I knew that. Drugs was just like drinking - getting drunk was always excellent fun and hangovers were boring but bearable parts of the job (even Bank Holiday Mondays) as long as you knew when to draw the line. Not that I really knew any of it, I'd never tried speed before, or cannabis or marijuana for that matter. The closest I'd come to using drugs was the Space Dust stuff which crackled and fizzed on your tongue. New experiences were like gold and rainbows, I was desperate to find them and to see how far I could go.

'Don't mention it - unless we're in court and I need a character witness, course. Then again, best for you to just not mention it. Right, the usual effects last about six hours and there's no hangover to speak of. How's that for value?'

I nodded eagerly. *'But,'* he went on, *'as I say, if you overdo it, there's big chance of negative crap happening. Listen serious Steve, cos I won't be saying any of this again, bud.'*

'I'm listening, I'm listening!' I laughed. This was almost like foreplay, so I'd been told. Drier though. And colder. And nowhere near as much fun, so absolutely nothing like foreplay then in reality, what am I on about?

He stayed straight-faced. *'Speed can make you extremely irritable, unreasonable and cause mood swings,'* like he was reading it out of a book.

'Bollocks, you piece of shit, you're talking out of your backside!' I snapped. Then, 'S*orry, I love you man.'*

'Right,' he said, as if ticking off an imaginary questionnaire, *'there's no danger of any of that affecting you then, that's obvious. But it can make you depressed and suffer from memory lapses and panic-stroke-anxiety attacks as well.'*

'Oh what's the point, Nath? What's the point in anything anymore?'

'There's also possi...'

'Panic-stroke-anxiety attacks?! WHY DIDN'T YOU TELL ME?!'

'You're not funny y'know. Speed puts a strain on the heart as well.'

'I'm used to heartache me, I suffer for mi 'art.'

'And you might hallucinate.'

'Auntie Edna? What are you doing here?'

'You're still not funny. And it can cause paranoia.'

'Is it paranoia if you know everyone's really out to get you?'

'Shut up, you prawn. And finally - speed plays havoc with your immune system. Still, so does booze. Not that they ever tell you.'
'Is that it then?' I asked. *'I thought you had summat serious to tell us!'*

These were to be new influences for me, the drugs and that. Influences isn't really the right word though, as I barely touched speed from then on. True, I was keen to sample just about any new pleasures going in life, but deep down I really did know what was dangerous and I'd only try things like that occasionally so as not to get addicted. How many times had addicts said that, in the beginning, I wondered. But I felt I was stronger and more resilient to such risk. If addicted to anything, it would definitely have been the beer for me. Besides, had the lads found out, I think I might well have got a slap or two for my troubles too; they'd have been well dis-chuffed with me. And that's how proper friends should react.

My boss at the hamper mail order company, the office manager Eric Kay, was a big influence on me. Not always in the positive sense mind you, occasionally there were inadvertent lessons in how not to do things. He was a good fella and as the first bloke to join him in that office, and an avid Leeds fan too, I was effectively taken under his wing. He had loads of self-confidence which probably served him well managing the dozen or so ladies there, so when I joined, it seemed he wanted me on his side and to maybe even groom me as a future manager. His brimful of confidence also made him a little bit rash at times I thought, jumping to conclusions and jumping down people's throats far too quickly for my liking. Still, in a way, I envied that about him too, as I was always, always shy of confrontation in work surroundings. That actually made me feel like a wimp, counting to ten in my head or biting my lip instead of laying into someone. Regardless, the need rarely arose in those days as my colleagues were brilliant and lovely, even if a couple were a bit off with me in the early days.

From day one my favourite was Jean, she was just so kind and friendly; and cuddly. Not so cuddly as to mean she needed to diet. Not that most women there needed to diet in fact; and not that it stopped most of the women I ever worked with from constantly dieting either. When the girl training me - Denise she was called (still is I bet) - slagged me off for making another silly mistake, Jean told her off for picking on me. Me and Denise became good friends too, funnily enough. Apparently, I actually made Jean's day once. Into the office she walked, looking a bit flustered and upset. I hadn't noticed and, looking up from my desk of the open plan office I greeted her with a cheerful *'Good morning'*. Well, she must have needed it, she gave me the biggest hug of my life and a big smacker on my cheek. She made my month never mind day, and for a very brief time I had Dustin Hoffman-like *Graduate* thoughts whizzing around my body.

It was generally a good and healthy family atmosphere and the work was, near amazingly, enjoyable. Me, enjoying work - bugger me! *Please regard that as a colloquial expression of surprise and nothing more.*

We received mountains of paperwork and correspondence from hamper agents and customers, not to mention accounts sheet queries and order changes, and most were fairly interesting fodder and not just monotonous pen-pushing and key-tapping chores.

How come, if it's 'not to mention' I just mentioned it?

Also, there's something gratifying knowing you're raising profits for an employer you actually like who actually looks after you. The best thing about it was that the hamper agents and customers only occasionally telephoned, as the number wasn't advertised so we didn't have to speak to them much. Obvious really that, thinking about it. It would only be a matter of time before they did phone in but those were the pre-call centre / battery farm days and before commercial free phone numbers even existed. Agents wrote in using their supplied company stationery and brown pre-paid envelopes in their thousands. I tell you, the postmen of South Leeds worked hard, there was no doubt about that. Too hard perhaps, remembering some of the 'letters' we received. One time, some sicko sent an envelope full of dog shit. No, seriously. Well, assuming it was from a dog's bottom, it was definitely do-do, we weren't too interested which creature produced it. Funny though was the time when someone sent a housebrick wrapped in a load of the brown envelopes. It was kind of touching, thinking of the trouble the sender must have gone to.

* * *

Just like only a few years before, queuing up at noon for Leeds games of three o'clock kick off, we were at Leeds Uni Refectory way too early for the Clash gig. Not surprisingly, *nearly* remembering the amount we'd had to drink at Roundhay, none of us were too in the mood for drinking in the Faversham, the nearest pub to the venue. In fact, it was the first pub I knew which got one of them video jukebox doofers installed. A pioneer of a pub then you could say. The other lads had tickets, sadly I was on my tod in terms of ticketlessness. Until Big Nath turned up, as I said. He *was* originally from a posher part of Leeds as it turned out, but I never held it against him. When he'd enrolled as a student he got in with the Student Union straight away, volunteering to work in the entertainment and leisure side. He helped out with security and was made a ticket collector for concerts at the Uni and Poly, not at the same time obviously, so not only could he watch dozens of gigs for nowt, he got paid a little for doing it too.

I had a quick word with him, to ask for a ticket.

'No can do, Stevie boy,' he answered brightly, a bit too brightly for my liking, given the gloominess of my situation.

'Aw come on mate, I'm desperate! I'll give you a fiver, I'm not after a freebie.'

He took his time, for dramatic effect I bet, and I effectively sweated in consequent dramatic anticipation. He had me in the palm of his hand and I knew he knew it. What's more, I think he knew that I knew that he knew that I knew he was doing it deliberately. What a waste of possible knowledge that all was eh? Surely I deserved better, I'd been captain of the school football team; okay, the B team but still, captain.

'Tell you what, chum,' he said quietly, maybe remembering my footballing glories *'Make it a tenner and I'll give you a special ticket.'* Then again, maybe not.

To be fair, it wasn't such a bad price. And so I paid, and so he gave me special concert entry. Crushing the ticket in to my palm, with a tightly folded corner of red paper with it, he winked, *'This will make it the gig of your life.'*

He wasn't far wrong. The Clash I liked, but never as much as The

Stranglers or even New Order - it was the wrap of speed which heightened the buzz of this particular gig. Dabbing it as instructed on my tingly gums in the Gents, I was soon pogoing for England at the front of the audience with the lads. My throat was sore and I had a runny nose all night as a result of the speed but it boosted me with so much energy it didn't matter. I was giddy and manic, out-jumping everyone on the planet, nearly hitting the ceiling, heart pounding and thrashing quicker than the Clash drumbeat. Meanwhile, Rick took a disliking to a kid behind him, blaming him for the stretching and misshaping of his new Clash t-shirt, despite the presence of scores of other fanatics jumping all over, climbing, sweating, pulling, pushing, dragging, slamming each other. There wasn't really a need of a synthetic substance for me to get well and truly in to the gig, it has to be said. You'd need to be like Helen Keller to not be completely wrapped up in The Clash when they played, and that was totally no disrespect to Miss Keller.

The Clash were amazing, Joe Strummer was possibly one of the greatest living front men around, behind Freddie Mercury who to me was a god of showmanship, even with his unhealthy hankerings. Strummer was like a threatening, 'alternative' version of Freddie - or Jagger even - he had audiences with him from the off; you believed they'd actually die for him. Although he was quite small and not particularly striking looking; he had a magnetising aura about him. He was a leader, his persona drew you in, not unlike JJ Burnel in that respect although JJ liked to look threatening at you too.

The Uni was christened 'the sweatbox' by bands who played there. It had little if any air conditioning and you could see clouds of steam rising from the mass of heaving bodies near the stage at most gigs. The steam met the cold ceiling and transformed it in to water. With gripping Clash classics like *White Riot, Clash City Rockers, I Fought the Law* and loads more (K-Tel time again, not), the air was foggy with perspiration. From the ceiling, back it dripped, *poured,* condensation, on to the band, on to their instruments and on to the audience, like a leak in a downpour. Rick got a drop right down his back via his gaping collar and threatened the lad he thought guilty of it, the same one he thought had stretched his shirt. Heinz had 57 varieties - and all marvellous if you asked me, not that that has any-thing to do with this - and I reckon there's more than a few varieties of sweat stench too. At every single 'happening' gig you'd face dif-ferent types of body odour. Charming it wasn't. There were aromas like sour meat, burnt rubber, acidic garlic, soiled damp fabric, fish doused in cologne and the obvious beer and curry perspiration. You had no choice if the place was crowded, and thus ultra-humid, you were bound to get someone's sweaty back in your mush, or even bet-ter, your nose crammed right in to the sodden armpit of whoever was in front of you.

* * *

'If I were you Stephen,' Eric said to me in his little corner office, *'I'd apply for it, if only for the interview experience.'*
The job as Assistant Buyer had been created as the company grew rapidly and the Buyer's work was getting too much for one man (Mal) to handle. With the backing of my boss, my *mentor* near enough, I had nothing to lose. And it all seemed to go that quick. That morning I rang Mal who I knew quite well and liked, and asked him if it was worth my bothering. And he was another big Leeds fan, always a plus in my mind. Physically a big Leeds fan he was in fact, too - probably so from scoffing all the samples food companies sent him. *'Course it is, Steve'* he'd enthused. *'Put it in writing and send it for my attention at Temple House.'* The Temple House part of the equation might present a problem, as my present workplace was on Sweet Street in Holbeck, to which Eric often gave me a lift; Temple House was on the Ring Road way up in Seacroft. Ah well, I did always say I wanted to travel. Anyway, I'd cross that boring bridge when I came to it, nothing ventured nothing gained and all that, like Eric had suggested.

Mal arranged to interview me for the job up at Seacroft - on a Saturday morning, of all times. Obviously it meant I'd have to stay in Friday night so as not to get out of my tree and painfully hungover in the morning. It wasn't obvious though, I was loving my socialis-ing and Friday nights were my main sources of entertainment. I needn't have worried. Well I didn't worry so I needn't have worried about not needing to worry. I read up on the hamper brochures Mal himself actually designed and I learned every single item that made up each differently titled hamper we offered; no mean feat. And, because I was a bit arty, I really did admire the way the contents of the hampers were advertised and displayed in those brochures, and I said so. They really were works of photographic art. Just because millions of things get advertised in thousands of catalogues and stuff didn't mean to say there was no skill involved in the arrangement. I said it all in the interview with Mal, and it all seemed to go very well. So well in fact, that not only did he give me a lift home he took me for a couple of pints in the Wellington too, before we went our separate ways in preparation for the Leeds-Chelsea game that afternoon. We both had too much cracking Tetley Bitter and come half time of the match, I sat down on the Kop terrace, rested my head on my arms and knees and had a twenty-minute snooze. I should have made it longer, it was a crap, virtually meaningless one all draw.

* * *

When the Sex Pistols were getting banned all over the UK in Silver Jubilee year I was firing missiles of deceased TB all over the region. All another tale. I'd loved to have seen the Pistols play but the chance never properly arose by the time my audio taste buds had grown out of The Wombles. The Pistols did play Leeds at least once apparently though how well it went down I never knew.
Do they call a load of baby Wombles a litter?
Rumour had it that Claire Grogan, the cute singer of Altered Images, got cut with a glass on her face at that Pistols gig and scarred. It might have been another punk myth I dunno; it wouldn't stop me fancying her whatever, she always did something for me did Claire Grogan. Or she would have done something for me if opportunity had arisen. It never did, alas, though there was always hope.
I went to school with a couple of girls called Hope, strangely enough.
Despite the city of Leeds not being in possession of a major indoor concert arena of any worth - the Queen's Hall *tried*, to be fair - we always had reasonably impressive concerts put on over the years. And I paid legally to see lots of them, as Big Nath wasn't on the door for many. It didn't hack me off doing so either. How could I possibly grumble at paying to see some of the musicians who were a mas-

sive part of my growing up, of my conscience, and a big part of shaping and influencing British culture? Never could I have a problem paying to see my musical idols of New Order, Queen, Thin Lizzy, Iron Maiden, Madness, even The Mighty Wah and of course, the gods in black, The Stranglers, plus a few others.

Good concerts, genuinely good, exciting ones that captivated, mesmerised me, were like great films, transporting me into other worlds, other existences even. I swear, just like as a bairn at the Rex flicks with my Dad, I'd emerge from enclosed darkness in to bright city lights feeling inspired and euphoric, like I could beat absolutely anybody at absolutely anything. *Nearly* anyway, I never did beat my Dad running home along Old Lane. And at venues in Leeds like the Uni, the Poly, Queen's Hall, Tiffany's, the Bierkeller, the Warehouse and even the Fforde Grene pub, I'd witnessed and been an actual part of many great concerts when that all-conquering sensation revisited.

I recall dozens of gigs. And due to various states of out-of-mind I was in, I *don't* recall plenty, too. Live music, unfortunately, just like everything else, could get mind- and feet-numbingly boring. Anyone who played an instrument well or sang alright - whether I actually liked their voice or not - had my respect. Begrudging yes sometimes it was, but it was still respect. I'd have been hard pushed to play the triangle well, and that's no disrespect to triangle players, I'm sure it took skill and aptitude I lacked. But in my opinion (which was all it was, my opinion) certain bands were just predictable, run of the mill, un-original. It wasn't just that other superior artistes influenced them, it was like they were actually trying to copy them. Tons of heavy metal bands were guilty, and punk bands. For metal, Jimi Hendrix and Led Zepp were more than just influences for some groups. And the view that punk was totally new and refreshingly original was a myth. The more punk - and new wave - I listened to, the more it was obvious where some of the sounds had risen from. Listening to the lead guitar and drumming in punk, no way was it not heavy rock in a different form. Even the Pistols' sound wasn't beyond comparison. Listen to Steve Jones' lead guitaring. It's great - despite his claiming he couldn't play - and it's near as damn it heavy metal. Even the greatest group around (in my humble) The Stranglers, were influenced by The Doors and some band called The Seeds, though Guildford's finest did make some of the best and most original sounds around as well.

The Buzzcocks played in Leeds loads of times. I saw three or four of their gigs - for free twice thanks to Big Nath - and they always put on a cracking show. When I first heard them though, I wasn't so impressed. For one thing, they always seemed to be singing about sex and I thought that was a bit off, I was only a kid after all, I had morals in my naivety (typical English embarrassment more like). Same with hearing bad language in a song, it made me cringe. Rubbish I know, specially as lots of football songs had swearing in but music didn't need offensive language, or was I missing something? The Buzzcocks were a perfect example. *Orgasm Addict,* I mean, come off it, if I'd took that single home my Mum would have stopped home being my home. And, more importantly - when I thought it mattered - I couldn't stand lead singer Pete Shelley's voice because he sounded like a nasty, screaming Quentin Crisp-type. Course, it *didn't* matter and the more I listened the more I liked, his voice was perfect for what the Buzzcocks represented, who cared if he was bent? They were classed as punks but probably only bands like Crass, Conflict and Discharge really knew - or cared - what punk stood for. The Buzzcocks were just angry, disaffected young men, singing about the rubbish in life bugging and confusing most young men. Shelley's voice did sound effeminate and catty but so what, it had a cutting, vicious edge as well, bitter, sneering, angry, rebellious. Attractive it became too - some of the notes he hit, just about no one else could. It was just right and he *could* sing as well as snap and bitch, possibly never better than on my favourite *Why Can't I Touch It?* Live, the Buzzcocks were brilliant - they were the human epitome of the essence of speed, if that were possible, or literal, and they always worked their damnedest to put on good shows. *The Essence of Speed, now there's a name for a band.*

Steve Diggle was a lunatic, jumping, thrashing around the stage, treating his guitar with violent disdain. His sound cut, *scarred* into your hearing, and what a fantastic guitarist he was: sharp, searing, wild, soaring. Rock guitar at its best, well underrated the fella was.

38

I saw the Jam at Queen's Hall. I wasn't a massive fan to be honest, they weren't melodic enough for me, like they were more content to shout or chant, with whatever angry message they had. They did have some fantastic songs, regardless, and produced a few great anthems, anthems with clever, insightful lyrics. Paul Weller was always angry and passionate and that was a big asset. That night they played for two hours easy, with at least two support bands on before them: The Nips and The Piranhas (of *Tom Hark* fame). The Jam really gave value for money.

As far as I knew, Iron Maiden only played in Leeds once, at Leeds Uni, and I was there. I went with old mate Gaz in our last school year together. They were more than just a heavy metal band and they had a cracking logo and image which was ace. They played the record market really well: even when the vinyl within the sleeve wasn't to everyone's taste their 'mascot' of Eddie, a zombie menace, displayed in all Iron Maiden artwork, would make up for it. Their picture sleeves and album covers were worth buying just for Eddie. During that concert, *two* Eddies came on stage near the end, spraying the audience with dry ice from flamethrower-type gizmos. It was smart fun and a lavish ending to a lavish concert. Paul DiAnno their singer, put his all in to his performance. His voice, though not a great singer in the true sense, was energetic and strong, just right for a blistering rock band. They sacked him soon after, I couldn't believe it, and in my opinion they deteriorated as a result. They went massive did Maiden but they'd lost me and Gaz as fans on the way.

Certain musicians over the years have been influences for later artistes; no secret there. People like Elvis and Hendrix are cited as being major influences, and being pioneers of new sounds. Well, we had one such pioneer in West Yorkshire, though he hardly ever got a mention or much credit. He was Bill Nelson, original lead guitarist and singer with Be Bop Deluxe. When he formed Bill Nelson's Red Noise and later when he went solo, he was playing beautiful new sounds before OMD, Human League, Depeche Mode, Fad Gadget and the rest could even spell synthesiser. He had a pleasant if unusual voice and he wrote loads and loads of smart, original tunes. He was always a bit of an oddball though, and you never knew what to expect from his concerts. Not that he toured so much anyway, I saw him play at the Warehouse just once - it was rumoured beforehand he wouldn't be playing a normal sort of concert but in fact be reciting poetry, with mime artists and dancers and slide-shows on stage. Thank chuff he *did* play a normal gig because the Warehouse used to open its doors at eight o'clock with bands not coming on until bleeding midnight. I'd queued since seven, I was well hacked off and if a poet had appeared I might well have chinned it.

There were tons more great gigs I could harp on about, but there were some very disappointing ones too. Public Image Limited had snarling John Lydon insulting us 'Yorkshire puddings' all night. Wasn't so bad a gig though I suppose, the tosser. And New Order - I loved New Order; when it was announced they were to play at Tiffany's in the Merrion Centre, I was among the first to buy tickets. Tiffany's was a decent nightclub normally, complete with mirror ball from the ceiling and plastic trees. Not plastic palm trees by the way - which would have been sorry enough - but plastic *birch* trees. Well they looked like birch trees. The interior designer, responsible for those trees, should have been birched, whatever. Aside from *Blue Monday*, which grew on me - like spots grow on students - New Order had some fantastic songs. Although the repertoire wasn't up to the Joy Division years yet, it was getting there. The pumping drumbeat of their tracks gripped you, and couldn't let go, Morris was a fantastic drummer. The strength of Peter Hook's bruising bass line hit you deep down in the soul, similar yet totally different to the Stranglers', and Sumner's morose vocals were compelling and took you to a bleak but fascinating world. The pummelling bass and drum beats took you down with them, way down, and the vocals made you want to stay there, like an addiction. But then the inspiring synthesiser music would enter, lifting you up, lifting your spirits high.

Those beautiful synth melodies would come slightly later in New Order's career - they were not unlike Kraftwerk's to my maybe naive ear - adding brilliant pop glamour to the overall sound. I grew to love their bittersweet music, their dourness and their cold, cutting, mesmerising sound. Weirdly though, early on they'd created this negative, cold and don't-care image by barely acknowledging audiences, even sometimes playing with their backs to them. It's effectively what they did at Tiff's and impressive it wasn't. I'm glad they grew out of such crap because all it deserved was a riot, a good slap and the not buying of their records.

Kraftwerk were rumoured to be playing at Tiffany's too, but it never materialised. They were reportedly planning on using radio-controlled dummies on stage while the real group transmitted the music by satellite from Germany. Stupid thing was, we would still have paid to watch. The Stranglers played Tiff's too, and of course I went and of course they were excellent. There was always something a bit bizarre about gigs at Tiffany's but I couldn't quite put my finger on why, until I remembered black clad people watching The Stranglers from the branches of the plastic trees. The Stranglers concerts were always amazing occasions for me and hundreds more like me; *un*like me too, obviously. Their earlier stuff was perfect to my ears: the grinding, unique bass, the at turns sharp, sinister vocals contrasting with softer tones, together with immaculate drumming and scintillating, science fiction keyboard, their music took me to every emotion possible. Eerie, only The Beatles had ever done that before. Stranglers fans were just as loyal as Leeds fans, following the band all over the world, supporting them. I met two great mates through following the Stranglers: 'Toblerone' Jim and Turtle. Jim had an angular head, I think his pillows weren't soft enough. He and I watched Turtle break his nose at one gig too.

Turtle had been sitting on his mate's shoulders when he leant too far forward, causing his mate to topple over. Turtle landed face first on to the stage. And it was only the support band they were watching, the divot. There was blood everywhere; same with his nose, that was everywhere too - absolutely splattered. Poor sod, he should've pulled his neck in should Turtle.

Such was my liking for the band - I shouldn't say it really (too late) - but if I'd been born a lass I might well have aspired to be a Stranglers groupie, they were that good. I took great pleasure from learning that I had a fair bit in common with lead singer/writer Hugh Cornwell - CornwEll, not Cornwall - as he always seemed to have a runny nose just like me most of my life. It was odd too that each morning after a gig, not only were my ears ringing from the music but they were well crusty with yellowy white earwax as well. I collected so much wax I set up a stall in the market.

5   F. H. M. U.

Whatever Will Be Will Be by Doris blinking Day woke me. I always fancied her, mind, even if her songs didn't do much for me and the fact that she was, away from the world of celluloid, actually old enough to be my grandma.

Thank God I was born in Yorkshire and that Ma and Pa Bottomley brought me up right, as a Leeds fan. Doris was clearly a Leeds fan too, if possibly a bit confused when she was little.

When I was just a little boy,
I asked my mother 'What should I be?
Should I be Chelsea, should I be Leeds?'
Here's what she said to me.

Wash your mouth out, son,
And go get your father's gun,
And shoot the Chelsea scum,
Shoot the Chelsea scum.

A lad called Hodge made those lyrics up. He wasn't a violent sort but was from Beeston and hated Chelsea with a relish.

Chelsea, the boys in blue from the crapital city of the south of England; I regarded as a southern equivalent to Leeds. It might have been a bit of an odd opinion but that's how it was; and I had a grudging respect for Chelsea, it wasn't them I really hated, even with some of their fans being just about the lowest of the low. They hated Leeds supporters; they probably hated everyone else too, especially blacks and foreigners. Chelsea bootboys and skinheads with their right wing ideological views were notorious. 'Notorious' like Hindley & Brady, and 'ideological' like my bare backside, they just wanted to fight and bully, pick on somebody they could pick on, with immigrants and Asians being their favourite targets. Not only did it pain me it bewildered me. Everything about the National

Front and the British Movement and such knobmobs seemed just evil at the root. It was all rancid - the public image, the slogans, the dress code, even the leaders' appearance, usually a cross between a boy watching flasher and a greasy haired, overweight bus spotter, in a stained suit. These 'colonels' would let their younger knuckle draggers do the physical stuff while they tried to learn to speak better in public. Was I on my own enjoying seeing wasters like that pelted on the street with assorted missiles? No, I don't think so - sincerely hope not. What I couldn't fathom was these dregs roaring and grunting how gloriously proud they were of our forefathers winning the Second World War, yet not only were they trying to make themselves look like nazis in combat jackets and jackboots but swathing themselves in the red, white and blue of our Union flag. They were trying to emulate Hitler's mob with their red, white and black insignia not so long before. And we were expected to just stand by and tolerate the NF and BM dregs chanting their *Sieg* bloody *heils* all the while. It was always easy for the government and FA to blame the football clubs for the behaviour of their fans but it was wrong, the racist shite was deeper in society than just in soccer.

* * *

In the world of football it was Manchester United I always hated.
Why hate Manchester United?
Good question.
Why not?
Good answer.
My reasons: -
1   I was a Christian. Admittedly, I hardly went to church but I believed in the Lord, I was a God-fearing lad. Them at Old Trafford liked to be called the Red Devils for God's(?) sake *and* they had a cartoon Satan on their club badge to prove it.

1A   They wore red shirts. Red, for hundreds of years, associated with blood, guilt, menstruation, debt, shame, hell, The Sun and Daily Mirror and co, and the devil. And prostitutes. And Communists. And Communist prostitutes. And very possibly devil worshipping tabloid reading Communist prostitutes as well.

2   Man U beat Leeds to the League Championship title in 1965, on goal average. Goal *average*.

3   More serious: Munich 1958 - a plane crash, with many casualties and the club nearly dying as a result. Horrible, mind-blowingly traumatic, you wouldn't wish it on anyone. Not anyone. And no one, *no one,* would have been sick enough to celebrate when it happened; the whole country will have been in mourning. Respect to all involved, I mean it. But it seems the mourning and sympathy never stopped. Ever since, it was as if supporting any team other than Manchester United was wrong. Whenever they were beaten, it was apparently only due to the great players they'd lost, no matter how well the opponents had played. And if they won, well it was their divine right to do so, naturally. Opposing teams couldn't win and Man United, well they simply could not lose.

4   They're from Lancashire - well, the club and employees are based there at least - and we, praise be, are in Yorkshire (Jerusalem) - therefore it was natural for us to be against each other.

4A   And for centuries they've stolen and taken unspeakable advantage of our sheep.

5   For some reason, commentators, pundits and newsreaders simply called them 'United'. The halfwits needed to realise there are other Uniteds around. There was only one Beethoven, one Laurel and one Hardy and one Winston Churchill but there never has been only one United.

6   During the glorious days when they were in Division Two, Man U supporters travelled around the country wreaking havoc - with hardly a word of objection or punishment from the authorities. When Leeds fans kicked off, the *club* was banned by the FA and there were government calls for LUFC to be actually closed down.

There was a definite need to clarify on 'hate', in case anyone thought I lost sleep with such rancour and bitterness coursing through my veins. Yes, I always wanted Man United to lose every game in shamefully inept manner, and to consistently and extravagantly waste their cash on rubbish players, and I even wanted their better players to get injured (yes, they did occasionally have half decent players). But I never wanted anyone to die or get seriously hurt. Celebration of people suffering never did anyone any good, whatever way you look at it.

There was actually a 7th point (twofold) for my hating Man U. I know many Leeds fans had lists of reasons longer than Georgie Best's bar tab but I had to draw the line somewhere. Leeds United was not in the fantastic shape people probably believed in the early to mid-70's. For one thing, there wasn't enough footballing talent coming through from the Junior ranks. Only a few made an impact on the first team; the star players were pushed nowhere near hard enough and consequently the results often should have been better. You only had to look at Man U for proof: European Champions in 1968, relegated in 1974. What a tragic waste, almost.

Two lads at Leeds who *had* made their mark and seemed destined for great achievement were Scots Joe Jordan and Gordon McQueen. They'd both played crucial parts in Leeds' brilliant Championship win of 1974. Jordan, who looked like a demented vampire flying round the field without his two front teeth, was a sound replacement for the great Mick Jones. He wasn't as skilful but he was just as brave and possibly better in the air, which took some real doing. What he lacked in finesse he made up for in guts and graft, plus, despite his teeth, he had better luck with injuries than Jones. And McQueen was a perfect successor to Jack Charlton, our one World Cup winning hero. Brilliant in the air and good marauding forward (admittedly with the occasional clumsy challenge or dodgy ball control) McQueen could easily have been another Leeds legend. Instead, they both blew it, by demanding more money. Sniffing their unrest - like flies around *brown honey* - Man United came in for them, with record bids, and both turncoats were soon on their way. Good riddance - that was one of the politer expressions - their treachery deserved our cruel disdain. It got it, they'd hurt the feelings of a lot of people, that's the plain truth and football fans scorned are a bitter breed.

* * *

Football could hurt as much as a failed love affair. Worse, the pain of football very possibly, if you were maudlin enough to let it, lasted longer. Maudlin, guilty as charged was I, it took ages for me to properly get over the relegation at West Brom trauma. Okay, I might have had a bad time of it on that sorry night but there were plenty of people took it worse. What made it really bad for me was that for all the time we were in Division Two, Man U were above us in the First. That truly did hurt. And Leeds' displays in the Second Division did little to brighten the gloom. Our optimism of bouncing straight back up to Division One was just fantasising, the players were never really up to it, too many let us down. True, plenty of things went against us: injuries, suspensions, the authorities. For me, one injury epitomised the whole decay of the club: Gary Hamson. He looked a cracking player when he joined Leeds from Sheffield United. He was left footed, energetic, could tackle and struck a ball sweetly. He was one of the few bright spots to the relegation year but he knackered his knee up in the last game of the season and was never the same player again. Such bad luck, and he was only young. I thought he could have gone all the way. Another very different example of great potential was Peter Barnes.

Peter Barnes was too good to be playing in a lower league, it was pretty obvious. But he should have trounced opposing defenders to prove it rather than look bemused with it all. You could feel sorry for him though, as he clearly came to Leeds with high hopes. He could never tackle to save his life yet he was suddenly expected to tackle and chase back, duties alien to him. He could have been a world-beater could Barnes, that's why Sniffer bought him, as supplier of goal chances but it never worked out as planned. Some games company brought out this sort of football toy thing to help kids improve their soccer skills. It was advertised on telly, in *Shoot!* and the lot; and they called it something like *'The Peter Barnes Sort of Football Toy Thing to Improve Kids' Skills'* gizmo. Okay, maybe not. All it really was was a football stuck to a piece of string which you attached to your ankle. Therefore, when your football juggling skill let you down, you didn't have to walk too far to fag the ball. Unless of course, your foot flew off with it in one of those terrible, tragic accidents you (don't) hear about.

Barnesy probably was manager Allan Clarke's biggest mistake, a jinx just about. He signed him for nearly a million quid, to provide ammunition for the strikers and thus win more games. In that relegation season Leeds had a pretty good defensive record but it was ruined by the lack of goals for. Barnesy was meant to be the crucial Part A of Clarke's attacking masterplan, Part B would be a powerhouse centre forward. Garry Thompson at Coventry City fit the bill perfectly. Others were mentioned too: Andy Gray, Tony Woodcock and, ironically, Joe Jordan, now playing in Italy. Great in the air, quick and robust, Thompson was a real handful for any defender. Apparently, signing him was all set to go through for around half a million smackers and so the rebuilding plans would be near completion: Leeds would be a major force again. But then Dave Sexton took over at Coventry and cancelled the deal. And Andy Gray not coming to Leeds from Wolves, that was another ingredient in the recipe of LUFC disaster. It was reportedly all ready to go through: a swap deal with Arthur Graham leaving Leeds and Gray coming here. But Leeds fans loved Arthur and demanded he stay, whatever the situation. Andy Gray would have kept Leeds up, absolutely no doubt about it. Graham *was* great though, he always ran his socks off for the whites.

The team's performances in the 80's weren't always worthy of being slagged off, we always had an at least decent home record but the away games were often long (and short as well) journeys of misery and boredom. In the first season in the Second Division, Leeds drew twenty-one games, exactly half the number of league games played. That was way too many for any club with serious ambitions of promotion. Teams playing host to Leeds did actually treat the matches as their cup final, it wasn't just a pointless cliché, the games often were very hard battles. Unfortunately, certain Leeds players seemed to look forward to their changing room cup of tea more than a cup final tussle. It wasn't all bad news, there were some good young players coming through in to the first team, to join some of the good older ones.

There was a little striker with massive thighs called Tommy Wright for instance, fast as hell he was. And before him, Aidan Butterworth and Terry Connor up front, not the most skilful players but they were honest grafters who gave their all for the club. It was a real shame when Connor left incidentally, not only because any racist halfwit fans will have perversely seen it as a victory but also because Connor was Leeds born and bred and a popular lad. We got Andy Ritchie from Brighton in return though so it wasn't so bad but Connor was missed, bless him.

And talking of popular, certainly in South Leeds as he was from there, would enter a strapping lad who could play centre-half or centre-forward: Peter Swan. He'd go on to do a sterling job for Leeds, in either position. In '83 a midfielder would begin a great career, an Irish lad called John Sheridan. He had class did Shez, one of the best passers of a ball around, though admittedly he wasn't the hardest working or the hardest tackling. Having said that, I did see him break his leg, away at Barnsley I think it was. He became a Leeds United idol because he could turn a game in our favour. We'd see him knocking around town in various pubs and clubs too. He played in two thirds of the games in that first season; whereas he was ever present in Madison's nightclub it seemed. He liked his beer as much as most Leeds supporters it was obvious, his game wasn't affected though. One of the Headingley boys, Dodds, always used to offer to buy Sheridan a pint. And they weren't cheap in nightclubs. Shez never declined the offer either, as far as I was aware. 'Aware' - not very appropriate a description when I was in Mad's, I was always a multiple of three sheets to the wind. I was never alone in that category.

There was always something appealing about sharing a drink and conversation with football stars, I couldn't quite put my finger on what it was. It wasn't because I was starstruck or in awe of them, that's for sure. Maybe it was because deep down, fellas like Sheridan were just like us, fanatical Leeds fans and from similar background. No bad thing. Scott Sellars debuted the same year as well. What a left peg he had, couldn't tackle his way out of a wet paper bag but a cracking striker of the ball. These good younger players, combined with 'warhorses' like the great Paul Hart, Frank and Eddie Gray, Trevor Cherry, Kenny Burns even, Kevin 'Jasper' Hird, *even* David Harvey and **even *moreso*** the later returning Peter Lorimer, filled fans with real optimism that the glory days might not be too far away. But it never quite turned out that way, not for years. Bizarrely though, those worst of times were in a way the best for some of us. We loved the new players and there was a genuine feeling of family around Leeds even if it could never be as strong as the Revie days. We really were all in it together, supporters and players alike, Leeds united.

6   Unspeakable

Down in the Tube Station at Midnight - The Jam.

He was built like an ape: big, muscular, savage look on his taut face, deep rough voice. I had no doubt he was dangerous. His cream Pringle jersey didn't soften the impression and his manner suggested his knuckles probably did scrape the ground wherever he trod. A feeling 'of family' with Leeds United supporters I'd spouted. Family my foot. This dirty, scummy dreg, standing yards away from me in the Kop, was nothing to do with me. He was nothing to do with any normal person. He was justification for pro-abortion groups, that's what he was, even if it meant an abortion twenty-odd years too late. What sort of filth believed singing *'Spurs are on their way to Belsen, Hitler's gonna gas 'em again!'* was funny, or acceptable? And we weren't even playing Spurs, they were still in Division One, and Belsen didn't have gas chambers.

* * *

All bouncers were bastards.

To rephrase - all bouncers *could be* bastards, certainly in that time. In my bitter (and lager) Leeds city experience, plenty did want to be. Within said bouncers lurked a spite to discriminate against honest and innocent lads, like my mates and me. It might not sound much to whinge about but for your night's fun to be fizzled out for no apparent reason except doormen wanting to exercise and abuse their 'authority', was as low as you could get. Any place where doormen thought they ruled the roost was not a healthy one to be. Not all doormen were bad of course, there were some you'd want with you in the trenches so to speak. A few were friends of mine in fact, like Patrice and Billy to name but two, top blokes who'd treat everyone right and make sure I was never in harm's way. I'm not sure why but it was as if they looked on me as a nephew or younger brother even; I wasn't complaining, it made me feel more popular. Mind you, none of this is to say all bouncers were particularly tough. Not that I ever wanted to test the theory. Some just wanted to screw up your night and the most likely way for them to spoil a night - if not a face, their hope - was to refuse you entry to the pub / club / *hole* they were guarding, without proper explanation. Or without explanation full stop. We were sometimes so low and undesirable we'd have struggled to get in to a Tory Party Conference, it was that bad. I was refused entry into so many different pubs and clubs in Leeds, I'd forgotten the number exactly, it was *dozens*, no danger. Whatever I looked I definitely did not look like a thug, even when I was off my face with beer. You had more chance of me hugging you to death than my hitting you, unless you were looking for it of course, and then you'd most probably have wiped the floor with me.

One black bouncer blocking my way, answered me with *'The reason is - we don't discuss the reason'*. He'd obviously rehearsed it too, the thick git. A six foot high, three foot wide thick git mind, so he didn't get much lip back. Well, none in fact, to be more precise, but what a tart. Perhaps they thought we were going to kick off within their glamorous palace of sophistication - like Martine's, Top Cat's, the Bier Keller or The Fresh & Easy Meat Market (that one never really existed) but I seriously doubt it, it was more like they'd confused prejudice and power with duty.

First impressions was one possible reason why racism was alive and kicking and probably always will be alive and kicking. Very sad but very true. Different skin colours, different languages, different cultures and different behaviours being thrown in to communities, needed preparation and planning. More than the authorities ever seriously tried, *integration* wasn't even a word in the bureaucrats' vocabulary or handbook. Of course, you'd always get hostile attitudes towards foreigners from *some* people whatever the situation, whatever year, blaming any problem in the country on non-naturals. Even students felt popular compared to foreigners. A lot of people weren't used to change and didn't want to even think about the prospect of it.

So, when many a white/black/rainbowed working class adult is ever presented with someone from another country, of a different colour and probably different faith, who they can barely if at all understand, distrust and suspicion surface. Those feelings aren't right but you can see why they exist. People are scared their space, their lives are being invaded, overtaken, by foreigners. It's obvious, and psychologically natural too I bet, that to hear a person speaking in a foreign tongue, your mental alarm bells ring: -

They're talking about me.

They want to harm me, I'm in danger

Or a plain old *They're taking the piss out of me/us/Britain* or even *They're plotting something and I want to know what it is they're twittering on about.*

The thing with religion and faith is mad. What people forgot (for centuries) is that worshipping whichever god you worshipped was always supposed to be **good** and **create** good. Yes, GOOD, not abusing other people and faiths, not persecuting them, not destroying them. Live and let live - all roads of faith should lead to a greater good, a higher power. I've never known which religion is the right one so I'm probably what you'd call an agnostic. Maybe all the various religions are variations of one faith; somewhere in time all the religions got confused and divided. Being religious in the positive sense of the word should only be beneficial for people, for us all, and should only do good. Being religious should make people want to help each other, straightforward as that, not anything negative. The trouble is, faiths and holy writings always were open to interpretation - and mis-interpretation obviously. This was where the psychos and extremists came in claiming 'God' told them to kill and torture in 'His' name. Faith's supposed to be for the benefit of all mankind, not hard to understand really. If I was wrong then you might well be able to find me in hell if you need me but at least I mean well, for us all.

* * *

That halfwit - and that was polite of me and probably dumbing him up - spewing his anti-Jewish drivel needed at the very least telling good and proper. I wanted to twat the twat, except he was older, much bigger and obviously tougher than me. Most people in the crowd were bigger than me it had to be said, but I was confident they thought on the same lines as me, that he was scum. He should have been dragged by the police to the back of the Kop and slammed behind the fence there, made to face the wall for the rest of the game and been battered senseless in the process. Well, more senseless, if that were possible, police brutality would have been acceptable just this once. Thankfully, only a handful of shitforbrains joined in the singing so maybe I was overreacting. And maybe I was being too self-righteous and standing on a moral high- but thin-iced ground, but whatever, I was on a roll and I did something I immediately regretted: I opened my big mouth.

* * *

I was no saint obviously - unless there was a Patron Saint for Hypocrisy - but I was never surer of myself than when against racism; I could think of at least six million reasons to back up my argument. And that need stuck on my mind as I blurted out '*Sick bastards!*' on the Kop at the Belsen bellends. And then I got neck-crackingly barged from behind. I then accidentally shoved people in front of me and caused a tumble of bodies down the terrace steps.

'*Stop bleeding pushing*' spat one fat bald bloke. Others jostled and pushed me, I was like a sodding (losing) Battling Top. And then, as I had my back to the pitch and faced up the crowd, a pair of big arms lunged at me.

'*Come here, tough lad!*' grunted the cream Pringle sweater bloke, his face now contorted even uglier. I was petrified. He swung a big punch at me, I couldn't dodge it. But ha! He missed me - I'd lost my balance again. His whacking great knuckles cracked the back of the fat bloke's head - two turds killed with one stone sort of thing. Jesus, I got out quick then, leaving the fat bloke threatening the ape-man and the apeman arguing, while other angry voices actually defended me. I flew down the nearest exit and re-emerged in the corner below the DJ's box next to the north-west tunnel. I stayed there for lots more matches.

7   The Singing Defective

Suspecting I could be a split personality was just what I thought about Leeds United and the fans. The brilliant Revie team could beat the world's best and then inexplicably lose to teams like Colchester, Chester, Crystal Palace, Sunderland and Notts County. That's no disrespect to those teams, but really, you know exactly what I'm saying. The fans were often just as unpredictable. The Leeds United supporters' collective was like an immense personality, a persona. It had different feelings, different attitudes and different approaches, but ultimately, it was one. I'll never forget - and to be honest struggle to forgive too - a very vocal minority in the 70's making Terry Yorath's life a misery whenever he played. You'd be hard pushed to find a more combative and harder-working player than Yorath but because he wasn't as good as Giles or Bremner, he had enemies on the terraces. Those doing the sniping should have asked themselves *who* (if anyone) *could* be as good as Giles or Bremner. The stick got so bad that his missus appealed to the fans to stop having a go at him on the front page of the Yorkshire Evening Post. He eventually left Leeds and did brilliantly for Coventry and Spurs - as well as captaining Wales a record number of times - and I tell you summat for nowt, Leeds would never have been relegated with him in the side.

There were men and women who had been to hundreds, in some cases thousands more Leeds games than me. If there had been a Chart of Leeds fans I worked out I'd be at best in the top thousand. Not that I felt inferior and nor was I jealous. In fact, I was proud. I couldn't believe that anyone, even these loyal people spending so much more time and money than I, felt more thrilled when Leeds won or more pain when they lost. It was hard to express my feelings for Leeds United Football Club, not by simple means anyway, but the Leeds songs helped and by heck did I sing them.
We probably all did.

Here we go with Leeds United
We're gonna give the boys a hand
Stand up and sing for Leeds United
They are the greatest in the land

Every day, we're all gonna say
We love you Leeds - Leeds - Leeds
Everywhere, we're gonna be there
We love you Leeds - Leeds - Leeds

Marchin' on together
We're gonna see you win (na, na, na, na, na, na)
We are so proud
We shout it out loud
We love you Leeds - Leeds - Leeds

We've been through it all together
And we've had our ups and downs
We're gonna stay with you forever
At least until the world stops going 'round

Every day, we're all gonna say
We love you Leeds - Leeds - Leeds
Everywhere, we're gonna be there
We love you Leeds - Leeds - Leeds

Marchin' on together
We're gonna see you win (na, na, na, na, na, na)
We are so proud
We shout it out loud
We love you Leeds - Leeds - Leeds

We are so proud
We're shouting it out loud
*We love you **Leeds - Leeds - Leeds!***

Singing at matches was always a truly stirring sensation; I can't have been alone in feeling adrenaline pump as our chants surged towards the players on the turf. Roaring in unison, Leeds United fans were undoubtedly the best, the most passionate of all football fans. Liverpool were good too, no doubt, and probably all fans felt *they* were the best, above the rest. Even Man U fans deserved some credit (only a bit, course). With games all over Europe, Leeds fans of the 60's and 70's were blessed with much more opportunity than most to prove it. The same went for Liverpool, the two clubs had practically grown up and thrived together, hitting sporting heights as partners almost. The Butch Cassidy and Sundance Kid of British football near enough. With me, as I sang - alone but a teammate of the Leeds Kop choir - the words would rise up, making my face flush with pride and my body tingle. Hair would feel like it was stretching and I'd bristle like a wildcat almost. I'd near explode in to tears as the lyrics raced from my throat and mouth - the sonic spirit of Leeds United fans materialising in to the air.

Chanting, shouting, encouraging, urging, imploring, praying, inciting, pleading.
Sometimes angry, sometimes aggressive; always loyal, always loud, always proud.
ALWAYS LEEDS.

Today, like the rumble of a restless volcano, 'Champions of Europe' rose up from the human ocean of the Leeds terraces. It first started away funnily enough, at the Grimsby versus Leeds game on the first day of Division Two. We'd created a new tradition, a new cause. The chant would grow louder and louder, hotter and hotter, more guttural, more passionate, more *frightening*. I doubt it was ever bettered than at Grimsby but at Elland Road we always gave it a mighty good go.

The Right side of the Gelderd End would sing '*We are the Champions*' and the Left respond with '*Champions of Europe*'. Each would be competing to be the stronger and the more partisan. Every roared line was pre-saluted with a proud, furious punch in to the stadium air. Metal barriers vibrated with the chanting, the steel and concrete surrounds shuddered and reverberated, and the ground really did shake.

While Leeds had floundered ever since 1975, Liverpool never looked back, they were undeniably the best team overall, with surprises coming from a certain bloke's Forest side and Aston Villa along the way. And the blue side of Scouseland - Everton - were on their way back as a force now too. It wasn't easy being a Leeds fan, seeing a once proud and great club harming itself in all sorts of ways. I was sick with jealousy and resentment of any team that did well, as we steadily got worse and worse. But Liverpool, they had my forgiveness, I didn't have it in me to wish similar gross misfortune on them. Since the early 60's they'd been our great rivals, it didn't feel right wanting them to fail or ail, both teams had risen together and achieved great things at similar times. And of course, The Beatles and Ken Dodd came from there, and I loved them. Having said that, Cilla and Tarby did too; I could never quite bring myself to like them. And even though we won the title at their place (Liverpool's, not Cilla or Tarby's) they were more often than not our bogey team. They had this infuriating habit of popping up with so many crucial last minute winners or equalisers it was a right royal pain in the South.

'Bogey' was an appropriate description for Lverpool as half their players had huge noses. No it's true. Tommy Smith hardly knew what his feet looked like, his conk was forever in the way. Ray Clemence had a nose a bit like mine actually, the old Roman nose which roamed across his face. Emlyn Hughes was always in danger of swallowing his, due to his big and whingey mouth. Steve Heighway was no shrinking nostril either, nor Joey Jones, and then you had the king of conks, the man whose prayer-worthy proboscis put others in the shade (literally), the great Phil Thompson. And he had one of those daft perms as well. Kindly, the Elland Road Kop faithful always showed their appreciation of his magnificent hooter.

It's here, it's there, it's every fucking where,
Thompson's nose, Thompson's nose.

Clemence always liked to share a chuckle or two with Leeds fans. What a great bloke he seemed, and he was always better in goal than Peter Shilton, no matter what anyone said. Shilton *was* great though and I felt a bit sorry for him, those songs about his inclination towards Alsatians were cruel, and for the record never actually proven. However, I always did resent the fact that while Shilton let Poland's goal in at Wembley through his legs like he was Bambi on ice, it was our Norman who got the blame for England failing to qualify for the 1974 World Cup.

My Dad had started taking me to home games when I was four. It didn't take too long for the emotions of football to strike me, just like with any adult, even though I can't have understood half of what was going on. One thing I couldn't remember though was his singing Leeds songs to me as lullabies when I was a baby. Or when I was an unborn Bottomley an' all, would you believe. Fortunately, along with The Beatles records, my Mum still had the Leeds singles in the family collection, too. Just as The Beatles' *Your Mother Should Know* was the song which woke me from what I really thought was the Afterlife, old Leeds songs rang strange, distant bells in my hazy brain too. The jolliest one was *'The Leeds United Calypso'* from the sixties with the lovely cheerful voice of Ronnie Hilton leading and numerous *'Leeds! Leeds! Leeds!'* from the players as backing chants. I bet I was *Leeds Leeds Leeds-ing* before I was goo-goo-gooing in my cot and poo-poo-pooing in my potty.

Leeds United calypso,
Leeds United calypso,
I feel so happy, I feel so fine,
The Elland Road lads are pals of mine (a-ha).

Now everybody come along with me,
To Elland Road and sing joyfully,
A lot of happy footballers you will see,
The pride of the directors and Don Revie.

It's the Leeds United calypso (sing it now),
Leeds United calypso,
I feel so happy, I feel so fine,
The lads at Elland Road are pals of mine (a-ha).

Now matches have come and matches have gone,
And at last we're happy in Division One,

Instead of the Mersey and the Liverpool sound.
We've got a special noise at the Elland Road ground.

It's the Leeds United calypso (sing it now),
Leeds United calypso,
I feel so happy, I feel so fine,
The lads at Elland Road are pals of mine (a-ha).

We've got Englishmen and Irishmen and Scotsmen too,
And our goalie called Sprake from Wales mark you,
Albert Johanneson is one of the few,
I don't know where he comes from, but I think it's Timbukto!

It's the Leeds United calypso (sing it now),
Leeds United calypso,
I feel so happy, I feel so fine,
The lads at Elland Road are pals of mine (a-ha).

Now all the Leeds supporters are feeling grand,
They're also very happy in Sunderland,
Records have been broken for all to see,
So buy this record from the lads and me.

It's called the Leeds United calypso (buy it now),
Leeds United calypso,
I feel so happy I feel so fine,
The lads at Elland Road are pals of mine.

Leeds! Leeds! Leeds! Leeds!

Supporting, loving a club isn't a competition, I couldn't prove I felt more or less for my club than any one else, just like parents can't prove they love one of their sprogs more than another. Not that they should ever want to. Followers of Leeds United were my brothers and sisters, my family. True, we 'lost' many from the family in the 80's due to the lower quality of football on offer but it was still a big community. Other than natural family life I couldn't think of a stronger bond, a better sensation of belonging than being on the terraces pushing for the same aim with friends and thousands of people I'd never met before but who I was allied with. Not even in the changing rooms before a big match for the Flatts. This feeling of kinship was nurtured at Cross Flatts when I was six or seven. Seriously it did, during assemblies the teachers had us singing Leeds songs on a Friday morning before another big weekend Leeds game. They'd even make posters of the verses and point the lyrics out for us to sing. Just like in pantomimes in fact.

Oh no they didn't!

On the terraces, in the streets, we supporters **were** a family and when the team or one of us was attacked a feeling of strength and unity came out - we'd defend each other. There has always been a dark edge amongst Leeds fans yet unwavering loyalty and mutual respect too, as well a brilliant sense of humour. Few things were funnier for instance than seeing visiting team goalkeepers running towards the enthusiastically applauding Kop, waving gratefully to the generous Leeds fans - only for them to respond, as he reached the six yard line, with a massive *FUCK OFF!* and countless V-signs.

There were fans of Leeds United in every continent thanks to the historical Super Leeds team. There were famous fans, infamous fans and normal, average fans living their individual lives in decent and respectable manner - and some the opposite no doubt. There were single fans, married ones, divorced and separated ones, fans who were parents and fans who were childless. And now post '82 we were seeing the Proper fans, those who stuck with the team whatever, through thick and through thin. *Thin? It was approaching starved!* There were Socialists, Conservatives and Liberals. There were Capitalists and probably Communists too, and even Anarchists. And definitely there were racists, just as with probably every football club in the world, like that scum with his Belsen bilge. Not as many existed in Leeds crowds as was claimed but they did exist, course they did. I never could understand it, men shouting obscenities at black players anyway, but when there were black players in the Leeds team as well, it was just mad. Albert Johanneson was black, from South Africa, and in his day he was a cracking player by all accounts.

So where the prejudice came from at Leeds games I never knew. **I** tried to be prejudiced - prejudiced against prejudice - and I've preached it many a time. But we'd all stand up and support our team together, despite being total opposites. There'd be disagreements and fights but they would be resolved.

* * *

Lee Marvin was a Leeds fan. Or he should have been.
I was born under the Gelderd end
I was born under the Gelderd end
the Gelderd, Gelderd end.

Knives were made for stabbing
guns were made to shoot
If you come in the Gelderd end,
we'll all stick in the boot.

Zulu, the film, is a classic. There's one bit in it where British soldiers look up to the hills as they hear the Zulu warriors approaching. Not only were they in awe of the enemy - even though they hadn't even seen them all yet - they were waiting, captivated to see what was going to happen, like rabbits stunned in headlights. And when we, the viewers, see the thousands of Zulus on the ridges, it's amazing, it's perversely awesome. I know it's only a film but they were the enemy and they were set to slaughter our soldiers. Watching it, your loyalties were almost split as the adrenaline pumped. And that's what it was like at Leeds away games: we usually were outnumbered like those soldiers, but we made as much noise and felt as powerful as the Zulus.

With every light came a dark, with every plus a minus, every good a bad, every Jekyll a Hyde. That was 1980's life - mine at least - and I had the choice to either live it or get out of it. Similar to beer being good and happy-making, I woke up feeling bad and miserable many a time after a Leeds game. And just like I was relatively proud of my own personality, I was of the Leeds supporter personality too, unable to justify much of my own or the fans' behaviour but able to put up with it. Sport was civilised warfare, played on a variety of pitches and surfaces with strict parameters, as opposed to wars fought all over the planet with very few if any restrictions. How could you not feel great being a Leeds United fan? We were often rubbish on the pitch but off it, we were champions.

8   D. S. R.

We had the idea to form Cross Flatts XI. Rather, **I** had the idea while
Mike (my one time best mate Gaz's elder brother) did all the spade-
work, like driving to the most boring football committee meetings
on earth imaginable and unravelling the lengths of red tape needed
(allegedly) to establish a Sunday league football club. I didn't hang
around with Gaz any more, or rather, he hung around with his football crew who liked to go fighting around the country at Leeds
matches. Out of sight he was but never really out of mind, he'd been
a brilliant friend to me after my Dad died and I'd never forget that.
You didn't need to see friends regularly for them to stay as friends,
friendship was permanent, indelible, unless of course some serious
irreparable fall out happened.

Mike often worked the spade on the pitch too, with soil and sand as
maintenance for the surface that every football club paid the council
much money to do. Ridiculous costs they were too, especially as
council pitches were free-for-alls, for the public to rightly use and
enjoy or just as likely abuse and destroy. It's never the council that
vandalises or ruins places, it's we people. Unless of course you
count Leeds architects and town planners as 'council', they're the
worst culprits obviously. And, seeing some of the white lines painted on our pitch, it was hard not to have a go at the council. More
than a couple of times the bloke who painted them was too lazy to
do it properly and so when he'd reached the goalposts with his line
painting machine he'd painted *around* them so each post had a semi-
circle behind it. Impressive I don't think. And many a time the
touchlines were wobbly, as if the worker had been drunk in charge
of a line painting thingymajig. You had to laugh.

Naturally, I was happy to take the credit for creating such a wonderful institution as a football team but I did let Mike share the lime-
light. In the future, when we were to be finally accepted in to the
Leeds Combination League, I'd have the official titles of Chairman
and Secretary Steve Bottomley added to other credentials (of

National Insurance number, Clerical Officer and my criminal record number *12XU* plus 'Drunkard'). Even better (work-wise) was Eric complimenting me on how well I'd reportedly done in my quest for the Assistant Buyer job. Mal had told him I'd really impressed him during my interview. Of course there were other applicants still to be considered but it all looked promising, I could almost feel the thicker wad of notes in my Friday pay packet heading its way to my pocket. I was under no illusions though, I suspected the imminent good fortune had much to do with me, Eric and Mal all being Leeds fans. Like we were freemasons nearly. Freemasonry was wrong, but maybe only people who weren't a part of it said that. There was something else too: as he spoke to me, I could tell Eric didn't really want me to leave his customer services department. I must admit I felt a strange twinge inside too. It was obvious why Eric wanted me to stay, I was the only other bloke in there and he'd miss the soccer discussions and general male chit chat even though he was about thirty years my senior. He was pleased for me as well of course, a bit like a mentor seeing his apprentice prosper I reckon. I wouldn't miss the soccer discussions so much really anyway, basically because they were hardly ever actual discussion*s*, not with Eric as he was always right when talking about football. Even when he wasn't right he was right. Millions of footie followers the world over were the same. He was probably entitled to be that way, being an ex-pro, even though he never really made it big time after a knee injury loused it all up for him.

Talking of breaking free, spreading your wings and the like, I was making plans of my own on moving out from my Mum's. We were flesh and blood but were winding each other up so much, sometimes without even meaning to. I'd have to leave one day and was realising sooner rather than later would be to all our benefit. Besides, it was only a matter of time before I'd get caught - with *wicked* intentions soaring through my mind and trousers - bringing some girl home, with my Mum getting giddy-kipper like, imagining whoever the girl was would be her future daughter-in-law. No thank you; it'd been bad enough having to evade the topic of why bath time had become my favourite pastime in my early teens without the need to explain the real reason for any chicks being present on a night.

As well as great player, Mark would be made our team manager. For all the hard work I actually did put in to the club and for how hard I always trained, he'd hardly ever select me in the starting line up, the git. It was just a good job I wasn't so childish and immature to let my resentment fester in to real bitterness, obviously. To never forgive him for such appalling treatment of a friend and miserable man-management would be cheap and beneath me.

Dodds had suggested, in all seriousness bless his daft punk head, to call us Fun Boy Eleven. I liked the name to be truthful (not I liked the name 'to be truthful', I liked the name Fun Boy Eleven) but it was noisily rebuffed straight away so I did the sensible (and spineless) thing and kept quiet. The best name I heard was G. S. L. FC. It stood for Great Set of Lads so trying to better that was a non-starter really.

Mike had managed to get a team strip for a cut price from Terry Cooper's old shop on Lower Briggate, Sport Spree. It was one of Umbro's designs, the thick white and royal blue stripes near identical to West Brom's home kit, and it cost about forty quid for the lot. Bargain, even though it forever reminded me of the horrible West Brom night, with my nose throbbing to add authenticity to the miserable memory.

Instead of the usual near chaotic confrontations on Cross Flatts Park against sides like the Cardinals, the Convicts and our old Asian adversaries who went on to form Beeston Youth, we started arranging proper matches. These were games against teams who amazingly owned such things as corner flags and goal nets and more than one leather football. As time passed and as Cross Flatts XI developed in to a pretty well organised and pretty good outfit - with accessories too - we'd play various teams from across Leeds. There was the Penny Fun pub team for instance, including very possibly the tallest twin lads ever born. They were nearly as high as Cottingley Towers, I swear it (not when they were born, obviously). And in their ranks was another big guy called Gaz who would, in years to come, have a permanent effect on my footballing 'career' - and more importantly my right leg - and not in a nice way either. Good bloke off the pitch though. Not *so* bad on it, in fairness, despite maiming me. Then there was Swarcliffe Working Men's Club, who would be our greatest rivals for a few years and on the whole became good mates, as well as Churwell's New Inn boys. On the other hand/hoof/paw were the Old Red Lion: cloggers and real dirty swine they were, intimidating and literally assaulting opponents all the time.

I'd never been to Kippax before. In fact I never really knew where it was. *In fact*, I still don't. I'd heard of it course, their Leeds United Supporters' Club was near legendary, and I *nearly* knew the apparent main man Gary Edwards. He was very probably the most loyal Leeds fan on earth and I nearly knew him because he very nearly chinned me, in the Kop in 1979, at home to Aston Villa. With a mate he was campaigning for 'Adamson Out', wanting rid of then Leeds manager Jimmy Adamson and chanting it all the while. I was opposed to sacking Adamson - I thought the last thing we needed was even more upheaval at the club. Since Don Revie had left it had been unrest all the way, benefiting nobody except opponents. Jimmy Armfield did a decent job - getting Leeds to the European Cup Final - but some people weren't satisfied with that and demonstrated it with offensive graffiti around Elland Road. He was, shamefully, just about hounded out by a dissatisfied minority. The world of football fandom brims full of opinions - that was mine, I wasn't trying to force it on anyone. Until that is, 1979 when, along with others in the Kop, I started throwing coins at 'the Kippax Two' to stop them chanting.

There were loads doing it, I wasn't brave enough to do it alone, oh no; I wasn't mad y'know. It turned out to be money not well spent. At half time, totally bloody seething, Gary Edwards waded up through the crowd, challenging each and every person he suspected of the coin lobbing - *'Was it you, coining me?!'* snapped in their face. I whimpered *'No mate'* when it came to my turn, feeling very hot and ashamed while something very hot and shameful touched the cloth of my droopy undercrackers. Gary and his mate's campaign would prove completely right all along, as Adamson was well on his way to ruining the team. Not on his own mind, it always takes more than one tool to wreck a football club but the buck stops somewhere, usually with the manager. Anyway, returning to this particular

Sunday morning, Cross Flatts had a District Cup game against Kippax Band FC. Some 'band': no brass, woodwind or even percussion anywhere to be seen.

Every player in the whole of Great Britain will have played football in atrocious conditions. Snow, hail, rain, sleet, fog, drought, swarms of locusts, you name it, they've played in it, and on all manner of surfaces, many with ridiculous slopes or mud flats. I once played for school at Roundhay High and there was a stone slab in the middle of the pitch - no, really - just waiting for some one to break their self on. And my teammate Shanny always enjoyed telling of playing on Corpus Christi's pitch up Halton when a knife was found in the centre circle, buried with the blade pointing out of the earth. Don't you just love life's scum? My favourite type of playing surface was always after there'd been a lot of rainfall, when the ground was soft, muddy even, but not too muddy. It made for the necessity of slide tackling, not that I needed much encouragement as I always loved getting dirty.

You should see my two-footed tackle too baby.

There are few better feelings in sport than being part of a fifty-fifty crunching tackle with an opponent - especially winning it. There's pain, pleasure, fear and exhilaration all at once, as well as the serious possibility of the ball bursting and your boots splitting and shin-pads cracking with the impact. There was a lad played for Drysalters, and he loved that kind of tackling too, except he'd deliberately go in late or aim high at his opponent's knee so as to inflict major damage. What a great shame it wasn't, what great sympathy we didn't feel, when he tried it on our Ian and snapped his own shin. His deliverance had arrived and boy did he squeal like a pig. We enjoyed it, no mistaking.

Our game against Kippax was on a public park, surrounded by a lane and with a small kiddies' playground in. A slide and roundabout and stuff were all in perfect working order, it was obvious the locals enjoyed strolls there and even the odd horseback canter. The footie pitch was in good nick too it seemed but on closer inspection players discovered the strategic positioning of crisp packets and polythene wrappers to cover mounds of dog dirt. They must eat plenty of roughage them Kippax canines, judging by the size of some of their 'messages'. Everyone demands large open areas for people to wander and exercise their dogs, but I've never seen anyone cleaning up in parks after them, those that actually walk their dogs rather than just let them wander the streets all day.

There's a lot of greenery, in Kippax, probably because it rains a lot, *out in t'sticks*, and it had been doing just that before our Sunday match. The pitch was sodden though covered in rich grass; all good news for slide tackle fans and even better for me seeing as Mark had actually seen the light and had actually picked me, at right back. Playing in front of me in right midfield would be Andy Baxter, or 'Baga' to all who knew him except maybe his relatives. He was my right sided co-worker, my partner (in crime) there to help me out in defence and for me to help in attack if opportunity arose. We had a good relationship, we knew how to back each other up in the game and how to communicate properly without slagging each other off or falling out if things went wrong. Things were always liable to go a little bit awry if we came up against the tricky winger types who ran quicker than the proverbial off a stick.

Fortunately, it wasn't looking so bad against Kippax, they were better than us in just about every department but me and Baga had defended pretty well and hadn't been burned for pace. We'd had scant opportunity to get forward though, that was the problem. The best form of defence in football is to attack, that's how we saw it at least, but chance hardly arose to invade their half of the pitch, never mind penalty area. Kippax were a good team, they passed the ball around well, battled hard-but-fair and the Flatts consequently barely got a look in. Their fella on the left was having a decent game but me and Baga had managed to contain him well enough. However, late on in the second half I lost concentration, very possibly thinking about nookie, as per, and I got skinned, him knocking the ball past me, racing to the by line and crossing perfectly for one of their strikers to score with a bullet header. That made it 3-0 and suddenly I was to blame for *all* the goals - or it felt like I was getting the blame for them all - as we had, allegedly, still been in with a chance of at least drawing the game.

He annoyed me doing that as you can imagine, so I vowed to make sure he wouldn't do it again - I'd make sure he knew he'd been in a good tussle with me. So, the next time, instead of trying to stick to him closely, I'd back off a few yards, waiting for someone to pass the ball to him. Then I'd have the chance to run at him and clatter him with a well aimed, well timed, well dodgy slide tackle. He did get the ball again and proceeded to run down the wing towards our goal. I set off running, ready to launch my incisor interception, to let him know, in football parlance, that 'I was there' and that I wasn't to be messed with.

The split-second dizzying blackout as I dived feet first at him, the soft, cool earth dampening and muddying my left hip and thigh and the brush of the ball on my right toes as I *just* made contact, before following through powerfully on to his pumping legs, was high excitement. He went sprawling to the ground dramatically as if shot by a sniper. I'd done what I set out to do. But then he got up again to carry on running, the crafty sod. And in between the sensations of my legs on the turf and my assault on his legs came a sickening awareness of sludgeness and stench splattering my right hand and forearm. I'd landed in a plentiful, rank and runny splodge of dog turd. It was all over my hand, it oozed between my fingers and down the sleeve of my shirt. It stank, absolutely stank, cruelly, disgustingly, I was seriously *that* close to gipping, the sharp putridity of it invading my mouth and nostrils and not easing off. I gagged, acid briefly shot up my throat but I beat it. Worse though was hearing players - from both teams - laughing at me. *Nearly* as bad was the referee ignoring my shouts. He *had* to stop the game, he just had to, for the potentially hazardous to health pollution I was covered in.

'*Dog shit, ref!*' I shouted again, hoping he'd see the perils of the poo and pause the play for me to get de-polluted.

But '*Play on!*' he called, running away from me, tracking the winger approaching the box. He - the player - dodged Mike's stretching challenge and whacked the ball low past 'keeper Rick's outstretched right hand from the edge of the box. It was a well-taken goal I couldn't deny, except no way should it have been allowed.

Outraged at the injustice, I just wasn't having it. '*DOG SHIT REF!*' I yelled. '*You shoulda stopped it, that's total bollocks is that.*'

He wasn't having it either, and he pulled out his yellow card to book me for ungentlemanly conduct. How I could conduct myself in a gentlemanly way while reeking and caked in dog shite was beyond me.

I looked like a one armed scarecrow, running around with my right arm outstretched to avoid the rancid stench. And when the left winger got the ball again and ran towards me, thinking he was Eddie Gray or something, complete with hunched shoulders, *'Sod this for a game of soldiers'* I thought, missing the ball completely and hacking him down again. Writhing around in apparent agony for a second or two, he was unfortunately nowhere near the filth. I should have put my hand under his nose like smelling salts, that would've cured him. Or killed him perhaps, I wouldn't have been fussed whichever result. I'd done my best to squirt the dog muck off with a water bottle, wiping my arm on the grass, anywhere in fact away from me and other players and kits. The Kippax lad wouldn't even shake my left hand, the sulking dipstick, as I offered an apology for the foul. He'd've really suffered if I'd pulled him back and left an imprint on his shoulder for him to remember me - and the dog - by; he should have been grateful.

'Two! Two!' shouted Rick in goal, meaning he wanted two in the wall to face the free kick. My aroma and I promptly strode over to line up with Baga. *'No, no!'* he pleaded, seeing it was me

'Left! Left!' shouted Rick, for us to move a little to the left.

'Get off, get off!' Baga squeaked as I tried to link arms. I could hardly hear him for his was a weak squeak. The both of us couldn't even stand up straight, bent double laughing, close to wetting ourselves. The Kippax winger took the free kick. He struck the ball well but at a height any normal wall would have blocked easily. Course, ours wasn't any normal wall and so the ball flashed over us straight in to the barely protected net. 5-0 to Kippax Band and the winger - the man I was supposed to mark - had orchestrated our defeat and scored two in the process.

The following weekend, another odious occurrence took place during a football match. This time though, I was innocent. Leeds were playing at Oldham's Boundary Park. It was rather slimy around there too and the match - as usual when we played them away - was pretty rank. So bad was it that Leeds fans had created a mudslide as a distraction and had begun skidding and careering in the gallons of sludge at the rear of our terrace. It was high-speed hilarity, much better entertainment than the match, and I enjoyed watching the development of the very first edition of the Leeds fans' *Black & White Minstrel Show*. As I watched them I saw Mal, our company Buyer, the man who had interviewed me for the job as his assistant, about to merge in to the crowd on the terrace.

Pleased to see him, *'Alright Mal!'* I called.

He looked around at me. In the very instant our eyes met I knew he'd already seen me and what's more had been trying to avoid me. He looked angry with me too, and though I didn't know why, I'd soon find out. He came up to me, speaking quietly but failing miserably to conceal his foul mood. *'You stupid little bastard! The job was yours if you hadn't assaulted that lad that night.'*

I was stunned, I didn't know what to say and proved it by saying nothing at all.

I had something to say on Monday morning alright though. Leeds lost that match and Mal had made my whole weekend even more a bitter defeat. Eric listened as, voice wavering like a right softie, I told him what Mal had said. I knew it was all completely unjust. After all, I'd paid my dues for my long-ago crime and taken my punishment, and here I was being persecuted all over again. Eric, who I'd obviously had to tell at the time of my court case, sympathised. *'Are you sure that's what he said though? Had you been drinking, maybe you misheard him?'*

Really, he knew I was telling the truth and I could tell he wasn't exactly happy either about what Mal had done. He sent me back out to my desk. Red faced with embarrassment as everyone in the office had sussed something was up, I flopped down on to my chair, dejected. The ladies made no secret of their curiosity, I could feel them watching me for clues. What I'd said about the company having a family atmosphere was right in many ways, proven by Jean kissing the top of my head as she walked by. A nice gesture but it didn't really help, to be honest.

Eric spoke on the phone with Colin, the Managing Director. After a few minutes he's called me in just as Colin is calling Mal in to his own office. Eric had switched the phone to loudspeaker and I heard Colin clearly at the other end of the line, asking Mal if our conversation at Oldham was actually what had happened. You could almost hear Mal's arse fall out onto the carpet as he denied saying anything at all to me about the job being mine. The fat lying coward. What a great pile of crap this was, this 'family' member I would disown and never trust again in my life. And eventually it emerged that my criminal record was exactly the reason I didn't get the promotion. I was practically distraught. No word of a lie or exaggeration, I'd learned from my punishment good and proper and had rightfully paid my dues. But now, after what Mal had done I wanted to have a relapse by way of giving the tosser a good smack and SCREW the consequences.

9   Sluggish

What a Wonderful World - Louis Armstrong. Judging by that choice of morning music, I think the jukebox of my mind was trying to be, how Septic Tanks would say, ironic.

1984, I'd finally moved to Headingley away from my Mum and our kid. It was a stronger wrench than I'd expected; I missed them more than I thought I ever would. It was though, a necessary upheaval, I needed my privacy like any nineteen/twenty year old and I felt like I was getting in the way as well as my Mum and Andrew increasingly getting on my wick. At work, I remained a Clerical Officer. By not getting that promotion I'd reacted exactly how a professional shouldn't and cultivated a sizeable chip on my shoulder. Even my Mum said I'd been badly done to, so I must have been in the right. Except I didn't show that much resentment because the wages were good. So I had a scowl on my face much of the time but carried on doing the work just well enough, with no extra effort.

With morning breaks I'd join the other lads (Everton, Kev, Chris and usually a minimum of three Daves) from other catalogue companies in the communal canteen, and not want to move. Me and Ev were the quiet rebels, returning to our offices only at the very last minute, unlike most of the robots who adhered to the Tannoy beeps like they were Big Brother-time. *'Stuff 'em!'* that was our attitude. What a time wasting couple of wasters we were. That was unfair a description though; well, of Ev it was an unfair description at least. He'd always seemed something of a real dreamer and it was obvious people hardly believed a word he said about his plans, aspirations and stuff. He did regularly spout on about packing the job in as soon as 'such and such' business negotiations had been finalised and I must admit, at times even I thought he was getting a bit like Billy Liar and his Ambrosia. But those negotiations did actually exist and proved fruitful in the end as he left to set up a trendy and successful menswear chain with his business partner Berti. I'm not sure how many people actually managed to say goodbye to him on his last day, as some were open mouthed with shock at his telling of the truth all along.

In Headingley in my new home, life was to be different, very different. As I passed a black-haired lad in a white vest at the top of my new street, standing on the pavement peering intently in to newsagent Freddie Fatfingers' shop window, it was different from the very off. He was too busy to notice us, humming and shaving using the pane as a mirror, with a towel around his neck and a bowl of soapy, steaming water next to him. I pretended not to notice as my Mum was with me. She was helping me move from our Beeston home to Headingley Avenue. Carrying heavy bags of my belongings she tripped watching him.

'Watch what you're doing Ma, my records are in there!' I could never work out why older generations didn't appreciate the things the younger ones treasured.

As we walked down the Avenue to my new residence, lying on the ground in the garden - if garden is what a ten-by-eight cement and paving slab creation could be called - was Dodds, a chuckling white spiked hedgehog almost. Fortunately, the sight of this skinny black clad lunatic with bleached blond hair wasn't as shocking for my Mum as the Gillette sideshow - she knew Dodds, from his working as a sparky for the council and looking after the electrics at the OAP Residential Home she ran. His hair made him look more like Billy Idol than well, Billy Idol.

'Oh hello Mrs Bottomley,' he said as he got up and brushed himself down (always presentable Dodds, even in punk gear), *'you're a bit earlier than we expected. I was just watching that weirdo up there having a shave.'*

The weirdo was in fact Ian from the football team. By the looks of it, he'd lost a bet. I hoped so, otherwise it was behaviour a bit too odd for me to take to. I still didn't let on to my Mum, she'd have only worried about what sort of bizarre life I was entering.

What was it about mothers and worrying? You could win half a million on the pools, save a toddler's life in the road with everyone safe and sound, you could be universally hailed as a clean underpants wearing saint, and yet your mother would still fret. Ah well, it beat them slagging you down I suppose. As I was always a bit unpredictable, eccentric behaviour was almost like *expected*, Ian meanwhile was a respectable office manager. He was an office manager for Social Services too, and he was only two years older than me. He still is. Shows what getting proper qualifications did for you. Dodds as I said, worked for the council, which wasn't as respectable as Ian but still *very* respectable compared to being a low rung on the career ladder (and hacked off) employee like me. At least I wasn't a student; being a *doley* was more respectable than being a student. Even being a moonlighting doley was held in higher esteem than a student.

My other new housemate was a lad called Dibble, but he was earning some Saturday morning overtime as a stonemason. Or brick basher as he liked to call it. He was called Dibble because he looked like Officer Dibble off of 'Top Cat'; I couldn't see a likeness personally. He did have a cartoon arse though, with the power to break trumpeting wind virtually to order. Not that he ever needed orders and not that we gave him any, he was a walking windbag was Dibble and often stank the place out. If he wasn't farting he was burping thunder-like. It was that bad, each time he went for a number two we had to put black and yellow Hazard tape across the bog door with 'Police Aware' signs. I don't know what he ate to cause it but on a morning, specially after a night on the ale, he made the bathroom reek of a bad eggs/sour milk combo; it was absolutely disgusting. I hardly knew him then but he seemed a decent enough lad, good for a laugh, despite his troublesome behind. A bit younger than me, he was one of those sorts who liked jokes at others' expense before actually getting to know them properly. A tad gobby that and not my cup of tea really but I could see the fun in it; besides, my being forewarned was forearmed. If he wanted to rub people up the wrong way then fair enough, it was his choice, he and I might have some good banter along the way. I wasn't sure how to rub someone up the right way anyhow. There was a cat too: the lads owned him, a ginger tom called Sam. Actually, I'm pretty sure Sam owned them but for tradition's sake, the cat belonged to the humans. Sam was one cool cat and he'd soon get his claws in to my life. If they made crowns and tiaras for cats, Sam would have been one of the first recipients. He was the epitome of the domesticated cat - *felinus moggipusstastic* as Warner Bros might have described him - and more. I loved him - we all did - and he became my favourite ever cat on the planet. He was so affectionate and laid back (literally, much of the time) that Cleopatra and co would have been on their knees worshipping him straight away, he'd have had them eating out of his paws. His soft little rubbery nose was a beautiful shade of pink, exactly the same as Squeeze's *Cool For Cats* vinyl 45, funnily enough, and his eyes seriously near to the same shade of lime of the Powerflex wheels on an old skateboard of mine.

From that day onwards and, I hoped, for as long as possible, 55 Headingley Avenue would see us having the time of our lives. If the respectable neighbours in the street (i.e. Leeds folk and not the students) knew what went on in there with us four lads and one cat, they probably would have had kittens. Ian's poker forfeit of shaving in Mr Fatfingers' window was nothing, neither was vacuuming the pavement or collecting waste newspaper from all the neighbours for absolutely no reason at all.

* * *

We placed my belongings in my room and I walked my Mum back to the 29 bus stop near the Lounge Cinema. Cracking picture house that, not as good as the dearly departed Beeston Rex but a decent effort. As we walked down the modest hill *(I'm an okay hill, just okay, nothing special)* behind us, a few houses down from my new abode came an almighty belch like the sound of a walrus on heat, then a shout of *'Get 'king tea on then!'*
'What on earth was that?' asked my Mum.
I dismissed it: *'No idea, probably a dodgy student neighbour, that's all.'*

My room was immediately on the left of the hallway of the pre-First World War terraced house, directly opposite a grey payphone on the wall. The next room on the left was the communal lounge and kitchen where we'd gather for beer, scran and the telly. It was small for one room, never mind two, and was crowded with us all there, especially when those pointless piles of newspapers had mounted. On the right were the stairs with the loo and bathroom at the top and three other bedrooms, two on that floor along the veranda, one the attic above. The attic was the spare room. Having a spare room was ideal. Well, not ideal exactly, it would have been ideal if we'd needed a walk in fridge; but as it was it served us well for our extra curricular sidelines. Originally, when I first moved in, the house was nice and warm, served well by an efficient if old central heating system. Unfortunately, it took gusts of wind of the strength of a cat fart to blow the pilot light out. Sam DID occasionally have wind but I think he was blameless in this respect. And so we were more often than not without the central heating. Naturally, the landlord declared there was absolutely no problem with it. Trustworthy and sincere our landlord, without question, never a cause to doubt him. We weren't too worried though - how cold could a crowded terraced house get, really? Well, watch *Ice Station* bleeding *Zebra* for a clue. Seriously, there were mornings when my windows were frosted up like a load of Ultravox limited editions.

In the attic, we made Lavish. The attic was the HQ, the fulcrum and the nerve centre of our operations. 'Lavish' the word - as we used it - was a Beeston expression, introduced by a lad called Taf if memory serves me correctly. It was used as great compliment to anything we liked and you couldn't really praise anything more highly than 'lavish'. In itself, using the word so many times in conversations was good fun and, well, pretty lavish to be honest. President Raygun referring to Diana as 'Princess David' was lavish; everything about Dallas, Tiswas and especially The Young Ones was lavish, Nancy Raygun falling off a podium that time was lavish (and a bit cruel I suppose) and every time Leeds United won it was, obviously, lavish. Quite rare like, sorry to say but lavish nevertheless. And not forgetting Leeds Rugby League club, just a couple of hundred yards away from my new home: even they managed to pop up with the odd lavish result. Not so Yorkshire Cricket alas, but we had plenty of fun there anyway, nicking in to Test matches and getting pissed while supposedly watching the cricket. I'll never forget Bob Willis the England bowler shouting *'Sit down you dummies!'* at us as we emerged from behind the scoreboard, illegal immigrants in to the hallowed land of Headingley Cricket Ground. With the daft way he spoke, dafter still long legs, sad saggy and bony arse and stupid Shaggy hairstyle, *he* was calling *us* dummies! The cheeky, weird-talking ball-chucking monkey.

Getting ratted, winning on the bandits and pulling were all lavish as well, naturally. Therefore, it seemed only fitting for a couple of business enterprises I dreamt up to be christened Lavish. With Dodds and Ian we formed a second hand record business, called Lavish Records, and with just Ian in partnership we had a t-shirt company named, subtly, Lavish T-shirt Company. The records scheme was easy meat - the t-shirt business was another kettle of er meat - as the three of us had diverse musical tastes and were well informed about which records were rare and so on. We knew our stuff and more importantly, we knew how much profit to get from each vinyl collectable. Record Collector magazine was our bible, and we used to advertise what rarities we had for sale and scour it for bargains, of which there were plenty. Ian had a car - despite everything, Vauxhall Vivas were classed as cars (*and* it was beige, for God's sake) - and loved visiting record fairs taking place around West Yorkshire, picking up the odd cheapo to sell or to add to his own collection (95% consisting of The Fall). And though we were in it for the money - obviously - cash wasn't the most important thing to us so we never split hairs about the splitting of profits and rarely argued about cash. Dibble even got a share whenever we did well, by way of a few free beers, and Sam grew rounder on his favourite dish of pilchards in tomato sauce.

Occasionally, I'd stop and wonder what it was about t-shirts. More to the point, what was it about t-shirts with slogans or logos on? I loved to wear t-shirts declaring such and such a thing, as if I was revealing a previously secret aspect about me. Predictably - even though I wanted to appear unpredictable - I particularly liked wearing Stranglers shirts; I was so proud to be associated with them, and Joy Division / New Order ones as well. I longed to be recognised as a fan of superior and gifted bands, there was no shame in that even if some people considered exhibiting your music tastes as sad and very 'out'. It wasn't so far away from the pride of wearing Leeds colours. And I was prouder still when a good t-shirt was home-made.

Painting t-shirts was more difficult and much more time consuming than first envisaged, depending on what design people wanted on their chest. It was okay doing them for yourself or mates but mass producing was a real grind. It was The Stranglers who got me in to painting. From the very first time I saw their logo - even though it was red - I fell in love with it. There were other undeniably great band logos around but none as good as The Stranglers' or their icons like The Raven, and the Rat silhouette. Ian made himself a few Fall designs and Dodds would wear just about any punk related shirt. What he didn't know about punk and new wave probably wasn't worth knowing and he must have seen just about all the name bands play live; I admired his devotion. Not that it ever really died but you didn't hear or see that much punk in '84 so keeping the faith was even more to a fan's credit.

In addition to the usual music features, the NME had featured Rik Mayall's 'Kevin Turvey' character on the cover. It was a full-page black & white photo of his face and made me smile every time due to his nutty look. He was blooming great and, more importantly, easy to draw. I drew his face on to a white t-shirt and used black fabric paint to do the shading and finish the portrait. Next we'd add brightly coloured slogans from The Young Ones, like *'Prik is a Wonker'* or *'I've got a runny bottom!'* in Sex Pistols blackmail lettering. We got six quid for each one plus postage; they were our most popular line and weren't half bad. They took ages to finish and I grew to hate making them. I enjoyed our other TV spin off designs more, the Batman ones. They were easier, less restricting and more colourful. In the series, fight scenes showed kicks and punches in writing in lovely coloured graphics across the screen, as kaleidoscopic doodle-like words like *'Thwak!'* and *'Blam!'* and *'Pow!'* and so on. Well, we used them plus some of our own creations, more 'adult' descriptions, in great splashes of oranges and yellows, reds and greens, pinks and purples, like *'Phooook'*, *'Twaaaat!'*, *'Bolloxxx!'* and *'Shiiiite!'*
What a *'Blassst!'* we had.

Not only did we design shirts but we also made up an amusing little scheme for boxer shorts. I'm not sure how long boxers had been available in Britain - they seemed one more copy of America the UK eagerly adopted, like twisted, crooked or senile leaders for instance - but they were definitely becoming more popular in the shreddies section of menswear departments. I must admit, I liked wearing them the most, too, ANYTHING was better than y-fronts to protect your meat and two veg. Y-fronts were always d-sgusting and v v ugly. Nothing was worse than a pair of yellow y-fronts with brown piping. I saw such a pair, really I did, at Middle School. *And* all-white ones too, which went yellow in embarrassing places almost as soon as they were pulled out of the drawer. Not that I'd know, obviously.

They *were* though more comfortable and practical than boxers. For example, with the close confines of y-fronts you knew exactly where your tackle was, so sitting down sharply wasn't too hazardous. Different story with boxers: there was always a chance your little soldier and his close comrades, with more freedom to roam in boxers, might be injured if you sat down too sharply. Especially in jeans, where mashing your spuds was a real risk. Me, I could sleep in bed with y-fronts on but found it really hard (not that way) wearing boxers. Boxer shorts 'rode up' and percolated my privates, resulting in well and truly overcooked taties.
I might well have said enough on this matter now.
So, painting slogans and stuff on boxer shorts, it was easy, a laugh and we profited from it too. Ian was a member of a cash & carry place where they had, amongst many other cheap things, plain white boxer shorts for around a quid a pair. We bought many, plus a spectrum of fabric paints, and set to work. Using appropriate song titles we created the 'Classy' range, and the ruder 'Not-So Classy' range. We advertised in the NME and Sounds in the small ads columns, a fiver a pair plus postage and packaging. Easy.

Classy	**Not-So**
Get A Grip on Yourself	*No Crabs allowed*
Nice 'N' Sleazy	*Vegetarian Girls not welcome*
Hanging Around	*Caution: Frequent Leakages!*
Germ Free Adolescence	*NO REAR ACCESS*
Slap and Tickle	*Beware - Heat Seeking Missile*
Stranglehold	*Make Love Not War, Again*

* * *

After cooking our own individual creations for tea one day, it was my turn to brew the Rosie Lee / Kiki Dee / Bertie Mee / Cecil Gee / Bobby Vee. Tea. There were white bits floating in the mugs as I poured, milk skin and such stuff forming on bottle necks was as common as red reminder letters on the doormat, abusive phone calls from spurned girls and Sam nicking your seat as soon as you left it, sometimes before.

'I'm not drinking it, it's disgusting,' Dodds. He hadn't even tasted it.

'It's just creamy bits from t'milk,' me, more interested in whatever was on the box.

'It'll be right Doddsy, get it down yer neck, yer ponce.' Dibble, gulping his own, noisily.

'Maybe it's the interior of the kettle, like the inner coating's flaked off,' said Ian, sensibly, you could tell he was management. He got up off the settee and crossed the two rooms in four paces to check the kettle.

As I watched the telly I heard him remove the metal kettle lid and pause to check inside. I really did think he was just messing about: faking the choking, putting on the gagging and pretending to be puking. In fact, after discovering whatever he'd discovered, he certainly wasn't pretending - the retching sounds were far too authentic to be acted, and much too long. What a waste of Walls' finest sausage and Heinz beans he'd made, now floating in the kitchen sink, liberated and unwanted (well maybe Sam might have).

Inside the kettle were remnants of not one but two chunky, very bloated, very hot and very dead slugs, broiled (or was it poached?) and light brown, each about an inch in size. They'd managed to slime their way in to the kettle and attach themselves to the inside like limpets on a ship hull. Somehow they'd remained affixed to the kettle wall during their sauna, but layers of their skin - or whatever it was that slugs were wrapped in - had boiled off to near ruin the tea. It wasn't so bad, at least they would have been organic. I felt partly responsible so I kept my idea of playing Three Card Brag, the loser having to drink all of the teas, quiet. Ian wasn't very well for the rest of the evening as you might expect, and he declined the invitation to join us in the Skyrack. Actually, I blamed Dibble for Ian's prolonged nausea, for taking two big gulps of the tea right in front of him just for effect, causing Ian to lose not just his tea but his lunch and very possibly his breakfast too. Strangely enough as well, he never wanted to see another slug in his life again either.

* * *

That night in the Skyrack was the first time I set eyes on a gorgeous blonde girl who gave me the proverbial tummy butterflies. Eventually, I'd pluck up courage to try and pull her, some time later. She'd barely looked at me tonight, but barely looking is still looking, whatever way you looked at it, and it was a straw of desire for me to clutch at and take encouragement from.

10   Creepy

The epitaph I always said I wanted on my gravestone was *'Told You I Was Ill'*, until I realised Spike Milligan had come out with it yonks ago. A better one for me anyway would probably be *'Should've Listened'*, because I hardly ever did. Loads of times, in my teens and in my early twenties ('tweenies' as hobbit maker Tolkien called them) whenever someone told me something, I'd often nod, apparently listening to the wisdom which in reality only fleetingly visited my attention. It would float away almost as quickly, into the virtual irrelevance of a lower league of my awareness. I always thought I knew better, or maybe more's the point, I wanted to sample whatever it was I was being warned to avoid. *That's* why mothers always worry, because, in the end, they're right to. Me, I sometimes worried about the situation with her, how badly I'd react if she got a fella to replace my Dad. I tried to relegate the thought as it confused me. I could never decide what I'd prefer to have - the easy life for me, no worries and with my Mum living with our kid, or her having a boyfriend and being quite happy but with me feeling left out and unwanted.

Speaking of unwanted creatures and stuff, I'd been reading about parasites and stuff, enough to make you lose sleep. No, I don't mean Man United fans, nor students and not even most Headingley landlords - but worse, stuff that would make your hair curl and your pubics straighten, stuff that live on and live *off* your body. Bed bugs and fleas were always bad enough, but now...

HEAD LICE for instance.

Head lice *(Pediculus humanus capitis)* are the most common kind of lice. Head lice are wingless insects, growing up to the size of two to three millimetres, and they live on the scalp. They have six legs and possess claws which are specially adapted for holding onto hair shafts. They are, not surprisingly, difficult to dislodge, the crafty little bleeders. They can't jump or fly (not without tickets anyway) nor do they live in bedding, furniture or clothes (come on, what clothes could they wear?) but they can be passed by close head-to-head contact. They lay six to eight eggs a night - 'seven' then in my reckoning - gluing them to the base of the hair shafts. Once hatched the empty, whole eggshell left behind is called a nit. As the hair grows, the nits stay glued in position. A bit like England's defence then in that respect. Grooming with a special kind of comb over a white sheet of paper may reveal one. It almost makes you want to go bald. Statistics have shown that at any one time 2.5% of school children will be infected with headlice. This can rise rapidly to 25% in an outbreak. Kids, don't you just love them? Quarantine the lot. After treatment for headlice it's important to trace all contacts and determine the source of the infection. If this is not done the headlice may come a calling again. I wonder where they go away then, on their holidays.

And then there's BODY LICE.

(Pediculus humanus) closely related to head lice but less frequently encountered. As the name implies, body lice generally feed on the body, but can occasionally be found on the scalp and in facial hair. They usually remain on clothing near the skin, and generally deposit their eggs on or near the seams of garments. At least they tried to be neat and organized then, that was to their credit. Body lice are acquired mainly through direct contact with an infested person or their clothing and bedding, and are most commonly found on individuals who infrequently change or wash their clothes (Man U fans perhaps). A change in to clean clothes and laundering of infested garments - especially drying with high heat or ironing - are generally effective to eliminate them. By the looks of it body lice are the dumber relation to head lice. But then again... epidemics of louse-borne typhus, louse-borne relapsing fever and trench fever decimated the populace through the ages, and millions more died from these infections during the 1900's during major conflicts and famines.

TAPEWORM.

Tapeworm infection is acquired by eating raw or undercooked meat of infected animals. Beef generally carry *Taenia saginata* while pigs carry *Taenia solium*. The larvae from the infected meat develop in the human intestine into the adult tapeworm which can grow longer than twelve feet. Tapeworms are segmented, with each segment or proglottid capable of producing eggs. That's just obscene is that, I thought *Alien* was bad. Eggs are dispersed by individual or groups of proglottids detaching and passing out with the stool ('log' to the medically uneducated). The groups of proglottids from the beef tapeworm are capable of movement and actively crawl out through the anus. Why? Where to? I wonder if there were tapeworm bouncers controlling their re-entry? Adults and children with pork tapeworm can, if appropriate hygiene is lacking, become self-infected by ingesting eggs from their tapeworm which were picked up on their hands while wiping or scratching the anus. This thus implies that many councillors, referees, politicians and British Rail guards are especially at risk. In addition, these individuals can expose other individuals to the eggs, usually via food handling. Ingested eggs hatch in the intestinal track and the larvae migrate through the tissues, where they encyst. If larvae get to the brain, seizures and other neurological problems can happen. This condition is called cysticercosis. NICE. Certain freshwater fish and salmon may also carry a tapeworm called *Diphyllobothrium latum*, too. The little shits can swim as well! Tapeworm infestation does not usually cause any symptoms and infection is generally recognized when the infected person passes segments of proglottids in the stool, especially if the segment is moving. Sick sick sick.

On to RINGWORM.

It's called ringworm because the worm emits an inaudible high pitched ringing sound when it's in danger. You probably sussed, I made that up. It's actually called ringworm because there's a rash which is ring shaped, with red or silvery itchy scales which tend to clear in the centre as the ring expands - it's not actually a worm, it's not even a living creature. Maybe I should have set up a *'Protect the Reputation of the Misunderstood Worm'* group, poor things, for student neighbours to support. The edge of the rash ring may be slightly raised. Ringworm is a fungal infection; infections like these can affect any part of the body although ring shapes are not always the case. Ringworm of the body is known as *tinea corporis*, while ringworm of the genital areas is called *tinea cruris* (or sometimes "jock itch" as they'd say in America - what they had against Scotsmen I don't know). This condition is more common in men, and produces a red (*red* again) intensely itchy patch which spreads outwards over the inside of the thigh. Ringworm of the scalp is known as *tinea capitis*. It mainly affects children and may cause circular patches of hair loss. The best known type of ringworm is athletes' foot, which causes soreness and cracks between the toes.

THRUSH.

Thrush isn't a creature. Well obviously it is, but not in this context, it's not a creature that lives on or in your body. It's worth a mention at any rate. In fact it's a common yeast infection that can be passed on through sex with an infected partner. Symptoms for men include **red**ness, itchiness at the end of the penis - treatable with an antifungal cream. Thrush is more common in women, and a man is unlikely to be the cause of the female's thrush. It's odds on he'd get the blame whatever, we all know that. If a man's partner does develop symptoms, it's worth him using the cream for a week anyway, and staying out of her way for at least a fortnight.

THREADWORM.

Threadworm *(Enterobius vermicularis)* is the most common worm infection. Both children and adults can be infected, although it is mostly found in children. Well, **I** never had them, I *always* missed out. The female worms lay eggs on a person's skin around the anus. This leads to itching and scratching of the area and then leads to eggs being transferred onto the fingers. The eggs can then be passed by direct contact, or through sharing toys, pencils and food, etc. Bizarre. Good hygiene is essential to stop the infection being spread, including washing hands and scrubbing under the nails before eating and after visiting the toilet. No, *really?* Now you know why you should always wash before eating. That actually makes me want to wash during eating. Or wash forever. Or just not eat. Or live in the bath. Eggs can survive in dust for two weeks, which may lead to infection by inhaling dust. Children in childcare institutions are easily infected by each other. Without treatment threadworm may give rise to vaginitis (inflammation of the vagina) in girls and women. You can often see threadworms, a one centimetre thread-like worm, in your child's stools or their bottom. *Please*; no more.

And finally, there's the Peter Sutcliffe of lice: PUBIC LICE.

(Rhthirus pubis) better known as CRABS. These small, brown, wingless crablike creatures, about two millimetres long, are usually spread from one person to another during sexual contact, although being naked and close to someone with the infection puts you at risk. Streakers were particularly vulnerable then. They need close body contact (the crabs that is) to spread from one person to another since the little sods can't fly or jump. Neither could I come to think of it, I hope no one made a connection. They latch on to hairs in the genital region and feed off blood by biting the skin. In hairy men, the lice may be found around the anus. The female could produce minute white eggs and any biting might then cause irritation. Irritation? I'd be totally seething. For others, who do not get any symptoms, they find out when they see the tiny lice crawling about in their pubic hair. During their lifespan (again, the crabs') which is around a month, each adult lays about fifty eggs. So not only were they horrible, they were horrible, little slags too. Treatment involves application of an insecticide solution, usually left on for up to twenty-four hours before being washed off. I think I'd wear it forever. Sexual partners must also be treated and all bed linen should be washed at least 60 degrees Celsius. Screw that, burn it. And the towels. Sod it all, burn the bed, the bedroom, the whole house and the person who you got them from.

There was no getting away from it, VD had to be God's way of punishing the promiscuous. I wasn't religious but even I, 'victim' of a sexually transmitted infection on my debut not that many years before, had a feeling I'd deserved it, even if it was my first ever jump. Like school though, due to teaching plenty of useless info - take blooming logarithms for instance (I wish someone had, taken them and shot them) - lessons very easily faded from my mind. Jean Jacques Burnel, kung fu-ing bassist and occasional singer of The Stranglers, brought out a solo album called *Euroman Cometh*. It was brilliant (I might be slightly biased I admit) and on it he record-ed a 'tribute' to crabs called, surprisingly enough, *Crabs*. I'd recom-mend a listen.

* * *

11   Hole Not Coal

Something Better Change by The Stranglers was my early (very early) musical alarm call this specific pleasant morning. Not a bad one to wake up with, by any standards. Standards: probably Beeston's finest band* was called The Standards funnily enough, and they did a cover version of it. Half decent it was too, though the bassist acted more like Keith Richards than JJ Burnel, complete with tab always hanging from his gob.

* Nods of acknowledgement to Nosferatu and to Roxana, before any of their band members decide to chin me.

I had a soft spot for Margaret Thatcher, our first ever lady Prime Minister. It was right at the bottom of my Mum's back garden where we used to bury the budgies and hamsters. The dead budgies and hamsters that is; I wasn't a Young Conservative. Whether Maggie would actually need to pop her jackboots for me to bury her was another matter, I'd've done it willingly, Tebbit with her. And with the saddle of his bike firmly inserted from whence his words normally came.

This is still in 1984 by the way. Not as bleak as the book but Leeds life had its moments, make no mistake. Our Second Division football club provided plenty of bad skies for us for example, with the odd rainbow or ray of sunshine to brighten us up very occasionally. We hardly ever lost at home, for one thing, and you could see a new sense of pride emerging in the team.

Away from footie though, in Leeds Market the rent was increased for stallholders and there was uproar and near riots. Personally, I couldn't blame them, there's something not quite right about putting prices up for market people, and it'd be the customers having to pay in the end anyway; as ever. We even had a drought, or so they told us. How could you have a drought in West Yorkshire? And talking of droughts, proper droughts that is, and not just someone's lawn getting a bit yellow, it would be late in the year when a certain Bob

Geldof and Midge Ure would create Band Aid and thus create legends for themselves. They deserved it, I was never one of those sneering gits who accused them of being in it for personal gain. Gods the both of them were if you ask me. In the Olympics, Leeds' own adopted daughter Tessa Sanderson won at lobbing the javelin. No one realised that she was actually trying to hit the Kremlin. Swimmer Sharron Davies (fit but never *that* fit) was to appear in panto at Leeds' Grand Theatre.

Oh no she wasn't!

What a tragedy of Shakespearean proportions that promised to be. I'd still liked to have given her one though, to mark the occasion. A round of applause that is of course. On a wider British cultural front, Richard Burton, Eric Morecambe and J B Priestley died that year, all pretty much masters in their own right. On a political front, there really was rioting, near Leeds Town Hall. Not only were protestors demonstrating against nuclear arms, they were opposing vivisection and apartheid too. And I think even some miners were there too. All worthy campaigns on their own - arguably - but some wasters felt the urge to vandalise the war memorial statues nearby as well; I'm not sure why. That crap was just wrong and offensive to everyone, not just the authorities. The vandalism and graffiti insulted those who died fighting for decent people *and* the scum now doing the spraying. I didn't think I was being too self-righteous thinking that: no matter what damage halfwits tried to inflict, they couldn't change history.

* * *

Our back garden (and pet cemetery) fascinated me, due to an air raid shelter buried under the grass, though I never managed to explore it. It was an 'ex' air raid shelter more accurately, though the reported constant 80's threat of nuclear war between the Ruskies and the Come-And-Have-A-Go-If-Ya-Think-Ya're-Hard-Enough Americans (plus maybe, Ronnie Raygun's favourite poodle, the UK) might call for its ex retirement. Me and Andrew often asked to dig it up but our hopes were always bombed by another overly authoritative woman.

We three Bottomleys had taken a Wally Trolley excursion down

London (*Larndon* to pronounce it right). We had a grand day out but Andrew wasn't too impressed, especially by our visit to the Houses of Parliament, just for a little skeg around. London has tons of sights and history, but it's a bit of a tip in truth and no one is especially friendly unless maybe when getting paid for it. I had my Harrington on and a blue Leeds scarf (you had to make the effort on special occasions) and who should walk by but Merlyn Rees MP. THE Merlyn Rees MP who lived a few hundred yards away from my Mum's, on the Wesleys in Beeston.

'Hey Ma, it's Merlyn Rees!' I called (to my Mum, obviously).

She was stunned in to near speechlessness (somewhat of a rarity) especially as Mr Rees heard and walked over to me through the few people milling about, a genuine smile on his face and an out-stretched hand. And what a handshake, he nearly crushed my hand. I always had small hands but my grip was good - but nothing compared to his. He was asking me where we were from and all that, and genuinely interested he seemed; I was surprised, in a good way. As I was about to ask him if Arthur Scargill was just a victim of media bias or an egotistical dipstick, Merlyn asked me, *'What the heck is going on at Leeds United?'*

Apparently he regularly got stick from another MP who happened to be the chairman of Notts County. Anyway, me and Merlyn sort of shared a mutual *'Shit happens'* shrug about it all before he went on his way. Leeds would soon enough get the better of Notts County, too. My Mum told me off for not getting Merlyn's autograph.

For any political belief or system to actually work, the leaders had to be incorruptible and loyal to the cause and the people. To get my vote, I had to feel I could trust politicians, much like if I were buying something second hand from some gadger. So it wasn't just that unnatural, sneering, condescending voice, or the horrible static hair-style or the unwomanliness and superciliousness about her, I detested Margaret Thatcher because it was the bloody obvious way she didn't give a damn about people like me, not as human beings any-way. *Maybe* as a number, a statistic, but that didn't count, if you see what I mean. I had until not too long ago been one of the four mil-lion or so on the dole. How could I give her my vote, how in my right mind could I trust that lot or what they stood for? I was a rel-atively poor working class boy who had always been against the

landed gentry, bigotry, snobbery, bottom banditry and Man Unitedry
so it bewildered me how anyone of similar background could actually believe Thatcher and co meant well for us all. And I knew for
a fact that she ate puppies and small children for breakfast too.

Michael Foot, the one time leader of Labour, was slaughtered in the
press for his not particularly smart appearance. Forget the fact that
he was one of the most respected and dignified figures in British politics, they didn't like the way he bloody dressed. If people cared to
look further than the piss-taking ulterior motivated *journalists* did,
surely they could see he was a decent, compassionate man. *Could*
but *wouldn't,* it was more fun sticking with and sucking up to the
bias and inequality of Mrs Thatcher and co and the shameful slimy
media. Sing if you're winning, get stuffed if you're not. I'd been
one such non-singing loser, I'd always felt it, known it even, and in
a strange way I was proud of it too. Greed Is Good and it was
Survival of the Fattest times. Well, I for one couldn't stomach it.
Whatever I gained in life would be hard earned, and that would
always feel better. She'd even taken us to war not long before, to
protect the 'rights' of a few people and sheep living on a group of
islands so small and so far away hardly anyone knew about them.

Michael Foot never had a chance to be the country's leader and I for
one was disappointed at that. Such was life though, Labour losing
General Elections felt to me pretty (ugly) much akin to Leeds getting relegated, it made me feel mighty sick with it all. I didn't have
sleepless nights over politics it was true, but it felt like a personal
insult in a strange kind of way when Maggie won. Funny though -
funny as in outrageous - that in a country always proud to decry mal-
treatment of pensioners, this older man, this statesman, was relent-
lessly insulted and ridiculed, and not for his beliefs but for his dress
sense. That said so much about how great Britain was.

* * *

There was only one thing worse than a workshy skiving student, and
that was a workshy skiving student with a <u>Cause</u>. Or maybe two or
three Causes, it depended on how worthy and *conscientious* they
were. Causes that were nothing to do with them other than provid-

93

ing opportunity to show strength and unity from up their own bottoms, they were the worst. A harsh view of students I admit, and not one deep down I *really* shared. Funny though, too. Students were always fair game for taking the mick out of, it was a crucial part of their education whether they learned (or liked) it or not. People were jealous of students, that's the truth. All that partying and staying in bed, paid for by wealthy parents or worse still, public money. And some of the 'campaigns' they joined, no one had **a)** heard of and **b)** couldn't give less of a toss about if they had've. *Pigmy Lesbian Single Mothers Against being singled out; Save the Slug; Organized Anarchists Against Government, The Garden Weed Protection League* and so on, and on.

All that said, one cause that definitely was worth bothering about was the miners' strike. Their fight represented more than opposition to pit closures and redundancies, it was the working class struggle throughout history against exploitative bosses and the greedy landed gentry. Well it was if you were bothered about it. Me being the contrary type (*I strongly object to that*) often overwhelmed with teenaged apathy and hedonistic pursuit: something was badly needed to get me proper riled about the miners' scrap.

There were some stunning looking girls studying in Leeds, and I'd never needed lectures in how to lech or lessons in falling head over heels for them. Remember, I was only eighteen going on nineteen years young. Every now and then me and a few of the lads would visit the Poly Disco on Friday or Saturday nights to dance and try and get a sniff of hot student snatch. That might make us sound like a pack of sex-crazed dogs I realise.
Is it just me or can you hear barking?
We **were** sex-crazed dogs much of the time, complete with flopping tongues and wagging tails, it was natural. Paula Walkden, who was studying English at Leeds Poly, was one delicious blonde dolly. I'd seen her a few times since that first Skyrack night and realised she was hardly ever far from my mind. With long blonde hair and eyes of blue, *guess what I want to do to you.* I later met her at the student disco one Friday night. Me and the lads liked it there as it was usually busy and cheap, you didn't have to be a student to get in and they often played cracking new wave records. It was all rather tacky

it has to be said, feet-stickingly so with plastic pint glasses and out-of-it students smashed all over the floor, but it had its merits. If things got too bleak and there was nothing happening on the pulling front, there was always a host of pinball machines and pool tables demanding attention. Not that I was any good at pool, especially drunk, and Lord, I was drunk as a judge that night when I met Paula. And she wasn't exactly sober. With drink came confidence for me, and my Dutch courage was so much I was nearly orange, wearing clogs and riding a white bicycle: I practically barged one spotty love rival out of the way to win her attention. *'Excuse me but I really really really fancy you,'* I said. To her, not to the unfortunate geek who probably was doing nothing at all wrong except standing in my way.

Paula had class, she wouldn't go to bed with me the night we met. She had a lovely face, even prettier when decorated with a smile (not that frequent, unfortunately) and the cutest turny-up nose I ever saw. Alas, she had 'issues', mainly with the government but also with us men and our view of women in society. *Bloody opinionated women!* We had a woman PM okay, but that wasn't anywhere near enough equality for girls like Paula. Actually, I agreed with them on that, as Maggie was there for herself and for the rich and not women in particular, despite what many claimed. Besides, she was hardly a woman, not in the natural sense, she was a manufactured Frankenstein Ugly. Paula was also resentful of the fact that she was attractive to the opposite sex (Paula was, not Maggie) which was already guilty of regarding women first and foremost as sexual objects. God did I fancy her when she got uppity like that. To convince her I wasn't a typical mongrel - sorry *male* - I had my hands full, and if I was to get my hands full of her I'd need to be pretty damned convincing. This wasn't a problem, it was a challenge, and I loved challenges - the thrill of the chase in this case. Her ginger mate Carla from Crawley wasn't bad either, though virtually always in a mood. Excellent norks mind. They seemed inseparable (the girls that is, not the norks, though obviously *they* were; well, I hope they were for her sake) and if given the chance I would not have declined the opportunity to see some one-on-one lesbo action, naturally. Paula and Carla were Coal Not Dole campaigners - the miners strike in other words - opposed to job cuts and production slash-es the government was intent on imposing on UK pits. They had a point, seriously: we had a government that absolutely detested the jobless yet here they were trying to un-employ thousands more.

* * *

For generations my Mum's family - the Bryces - was part of the mining community in Sharlston, Wakefield so I should really have been a deeply passionate supporter of the strike from my bairn-days. I *was* always proud of the family background but now I was a pen pushing city tosspot remember, and so I did very little bar shouting *'Yorkshire Miners'* at every concert I went to. Even that wasn't certain, remembering the state I'd been in at some gigs. My heart *was* with the miners that's the truth, and I had plenty of arguments with certain more right wing mates, but deep down I felt I had nothing to do with it all. For me to join them would be like my gatecrashing a party; I'd be a hypocrite. However, the pretty girls wanted me to join them on the picket line and I just couldn't say no, they had me wrapped around their little manicured fingers, the nail varnish having not been tested on animals, mark you.

I'd previously thought NUS was what I'd caught off the Halton Moor harlot until I realised it was a union, I'd got the letters mixed up. *Said the dyslexic potsman.* I couldn't understand why non-workers such as students actually needed a union. But to their credit the NUS stood up to be counted in their support of the miners strike. And the union put their money where their mouths were - we hopped on to a free minibus they'd laid on early one morning to Selby pit. I was going to stand and support the campaign, with the lovely Paula, she of the chips on her shoulder on my shoulder, and Carla in tow.

* * *

FIGHT, FIGHT, FIGHT! There's a fight on oop North!
The white-shirted Southern allies rallied to help their beleaguered blue-collared colleagues of the North's police forces. That's how most of the papers put it at least. You see, the scum (the collective noun for miners) was acting up, disobeying the rules of class and

nature and defying their role in society as decreed by Her Majesty Thatcher. Those hole digging, thick Yorkshire bastards needed a lesson or ten drumming into them and the boys in blue from the South were the very willing percussionists.

The first thing that struck me - more would follow, trust me - about Selby pit was how ugly it was. Why in God's earth would anyone want to work there? Selby itself was alright, it even had a lovely abbey, but why would anyone want to work *under* the ground *anywhere*? Christ, the claustrophobia, the dark, the filth, the risk - you'd have to be desperate to do that sort of graft. *On* the surface must have been bleak enough, it wasn't exactly picturesque or serene there either. I'd watched documentaries about the pits - never a more fitting description it seemed to me - and read history books to know that there was not a chance in hell you'd have got me working down there, ever. Not ever. Yet here I was, helping men fight for the right to do exactly that. Them miners I tell you, ten times the man I was.

I'd taken a day's holiday for the occasion. I was that right minded I'd have pulled a sicky if needs had been anyway. The minibus for our day out was hardly full. I was buzzing, chatty, up for it all and anxious to impress the girls. That was more likely thanks to the ale the previous night and a tiny bit of speed I'd sniffed to wake myself up. There were four or five other students in addition to camera-wielding Paula and Carla, and an older bloke who drove; he was about thirty five I reckoned, bald and wearing a duffle coat with a long multicoloured scarf. No really, and in late summer; I suspect he was a Dr Who fan, or just a bit of a nerd. He might actually have been a lecturer, even the girls weren't sure. I sincerely hoped he wasn't a lecturer in Fashion, that was for sure. Approaching Selby, it was clear the police were already well organised, like in a game of *Campaign*: scores lined up at roadblocks, checkpoints, gates and picket zones all over the place. It was like away trips for Leeds games and I felt a thrill, a hum of un-welcome just like travelling supporters always got.

* * *

And to think, I'd been brought up to totally respect the police. Weren't they supposed to respect us too?

I expected pushing and shoving.

I expected shouting and chanting and whistling and jeering.

I even expected spitting, cursing and bitter hostility.

I wasn't *disappointed.*

Those expectations were my main reasons for accompanying Paula and Carla. Privately I thought they were being reckless, immature even, trying to join a protest they had nothing to do with and where only bad was likely to happen. And in hindsight, taking cameras with them wasn't the best of ideas. I decided they needed someone to protect them. I was that someone. Admittedly, I fancied the pants off one of them and the other I wouldn't have said no to, so my intentions weren't entirely honourable, but there definitely were good deeds on my mind.

I *hadn't* expected to hear officers of the law marching as if unto war. I hadn't expected to hear a low rumble of *'Overtime, overtime, overtime'* from their lips as they approached other colleagues lined up yards away from dozens of pickets.

I hadn't expected to see policemen commence hostilities by charging down the street at crouching or sitting *passive* miners, or lashing out with batons, truncheons, reinforced fists and shields against any non-police in their way or even *nearly* in their way.

And I hadn't really expected to have to try and defend the girls.

I wasn't disappointed then either. No, I was stunned and eventually bloodied, but not disappointed.

* * *

'It wasn't your battle, Stephen,' she moaned again, *'and you should never have gone there in the first place.'*

I was back home, at my Mum's. I wasn't in the mood and I had a stinging headache. The instant that baton had cracked down upon my skull I'd suspected there was a moral somewhere just waiting to be preached to me. I'd been trying to shield the girls from the mounted copper, I just knew he was out to *get* someone and as the huge black horse cantered towards us down the road I sussed it might well be us, or at least the girls' cameras. Everything just erupted, there had been no warning sign, no indication, the police had suddenly rushed the pickets hanging around in the sunshine. A couple of miners jumped up and shouted to alert the rest but it was total confusion and we didn't have a clue what was going on. Men ran in all directions, retreating or attacking, it wasn't exactly clear. We didn't know whether to run away, stay still or what. Policemen and pickets were exchanging spits, punches and insults like it was a game; it was a free-for-all combat zone. The girls started taking photos. Men were beaten and dragged away by uniforms. And this one faceless copper on horseback had completely lost his mind, he *had* to find someone to batter. He looked like one of those Dark Riders in Lord of the Rings, he really did. Some'd say I brought it all upon myself, though I don't recall grabbing his arm or hitting myself on the head with his baton. Mindst you, I shouldn't have shouted *'Leave em alone you piece of shit!'* either, I admit it, and the girls shouldn't have screamed at him or took photos.

It had taken well over an hour to get to Selby. All the excitement and build-up had led to a very short adventure of a few minutes only. By the day's end I had one big, throbbing and congealed cut on my head and had reportedly lost maybe half a pint of blood.

'You're not an activist or whatever them professional picketers call themselves,' she added.

*'Mum, my head's hurting enough without this crap! I thought **you'd** understand.'*

'I do understand, but if you try such stupidity again I'll give you a bigger bump on the nut!'

'Bollocks.'

'I'M NOT JOKING!' she shouted. I stayed quiet, shocked at the rage, and ashamed, knowing she was, of course, right.

At least the girls hadn't been hurt and it meant I was well and truly in their good books, the headache (and earache) may all have been worth it.

12   Dirty Tactics

Relax - Frankie Goes to Hollywood.
'Don't do anyone I wouldn't do,' I quipped as Ian, Dodds and Dibble made their way out of the house one Friday evening.
'Not much chance of that really, is there Stevie boy?' chirped Ian, cheekily.
'Not much chance of that really, is there Stevie boy?' I mimicked in as bitchy a voice as I could muster, immediately worrying how authentic I sounded. *Too* authentic but thank God no one seemed to notice.
'Sure you're not coming out? I mean, it's Freedy neet!'
'Dodds, I know - and it's bad news but I've gotta do it,' I explained; sort of.
Missing a Friday night out was almost unheard of and it really did give me a churning gut ache; I couldn't recall the last time I'd done it, if ever. Going out with your mates was unbeatable, you never know what's going to happen and you're almost guaranteed to near wet yourself laughing at some stage in the proceedings. All unpredictable, exciting, lavish stuff. And tonight there was I, not with them; I must've been mad.

Over my early drinking years, I'd tried to be a bad lad many times, a dirty dog to be more precise. Before I met Paula, I'd had plenty of pleasant times of flesh once I'd got my cherry out of the way (and the consequent Vera Duckworth). Different size girls, different ages, different backgrounds and of course different names. Some I totally forgot almost as soon as I was told them, *slightly* embarrassing moments. Girls occasionally forgot mine though, too. Some of the states I got in, so did I.
'Leave him, the queer boy,' Dibble said, trying to wind me up as was his way. It never worked, or rather I tried to convince him it never worked, except even without his trying sometimes, it virtually always did work.
'Dibble, go shag a bird in a drunken coma, in a skip. Again. You freak'

'That never happened!' he said, with difficulty as he was grinning. He knew he'd be arguing in vain - we had him believing we believed the story one of his mates (JW) had let us in on.

'At least I'm getting some,' he added, meekly. No he wasn't, he probably knew we knew that, too.

They left for the Skyrack and probably on to a few more pubs and clubs in town. I was regretting my decision to stay in already, and the slam of the door hadn't even faded yet. They'd be on the pull again, the thrill of the chase and the race of alcohol energising them, while I was staying in like a good boy, hoping - and what's more, maybe in vain - for a nibble at least. They, as normal, would be chatting up and very possibly bedding new nubile nymphos. *Bring On The Nubiles*! Like I said, I'd quite often been a quality puller myself before, like a Keith Edwards of socialising, scoring at least once a week outside the top division. Lumped together with the fact my targets were often just as paggered and equally uninhibited, the sawdust beneath my notched bedpost had steadily increased. Until Paula, that is; then I became a one-chick pony. I even cut down on watching dirty vids, something must have been well different in me. You watch, I'd be wearing a tie next or polishing my shoes even.

As peace and quiet descended on the place, I went back in to the living room to prepare for my night. I was getting more excited than on the eve of a new Leeds footie season. Spilling Sam the Ginger Ball out in to the mild Headingley evening, I was surprised at how nervous I felt with Paula's impending arrival. Outside it was a clear evening and I was sure Sam would find some entertainment elsewhere, like cats did, even the chilled out Steve McQueen of cats. He'd forgiven us for taking him drinking in the Skyrack a few weeks before. The experience had seemed to bemuse him, which I thought odd, he'd always seemed the sociable sort before. We'd given him as much milk as he could've wanted for, as well. None of us got a sniff that night though Sam at least got stroked a few times by women.

Paula and I had become closer because of the Selby incident. She'd realised I wasn't just trying to get into her knickers and that in fact I was quite a nice and decent lad (even though 'nice' was always a dubious compliment - Peter Purves, Val Doonican and ratting Mickey Mouse were *nice*). We were seeing each other nearly every day now (me and Paula, not the above mentioned superstars) for drinks, kisses and cuddles here and there: around Headingley's pubs and sometimes even the splendid Vic near the Town Hall if we were adventurous and Paula had enough energy after lectures. Trouble was, certainly for me anyway, the *certain* holds-barred arrangement we had was making me ache so hard I couldn't walk properly. Or sit properly. Or even stand properly for that matter. And that's all we ever did, kissed and cuddled, I wanted more, I needed more. Fire down below - more like rigor mortis actually - was afflicting me very effectively. It wasn't that I felt entitled to be her first but I craved more, my body was yearning for nuptials so much. Reason flew out of the window when my begging loins were alerted, and I got very frustrated. We had come (I wished) to a point where in my insensitive male mind we should either get serious and get all over each other like bunnies or just call it a no score draw. I mean, we'd been seeing each other for nearly six months. Six months, a new personal record! If she really liked me, loved me even, then there really should be nothing stopping her from sleeping with me. After all, I was no sex pest and I'd demonstrated gallantry I'd never known I even possessed before. And I think I was in love with her, though having really not been there before, I couldn't be sure. Could anyone? Were men and women actually meant to fall in love, was it natural? It all mixed me up big time.

I'd not even as much as looked at another girl since we'd met, never mind had my way with any. Alright, I *had* looked but there was no harm in that, surely, and I definitely hadn't been unfaithful. I'd volunteered for nookie cold turkey because of Paula, and it hurt; I must have been mad. No, not mad, I'd been good and obedient, that was it, and this Friday night would be my reward, the turning point for our relationship. We would become one, we'd become a proper couple, no more pretending, no more faffing about. As I'd finally managed to persuade her to spend an evening with me in my luxury apartment, tonight was to be the night. Well, bedsit not apartment. We'd spoken about sex but, always noticing her shyness, I'd never really forced the issue (or myself on her for that matter). Sober I was actually pretty shy, despite what people might have thought about me.

Paula knocked on the front door at eight o'clock on the dot, holding a bottle of Liebfraumilch and wearing all red and a shy smile on her pale, lovely face. I noticed in her eyes as she only momentarily looked in to mine, that she was nervous. I'd warmed myself up with three cans of Skol and a sly tug over *Emmanuelle* on video. Sorry, I couldn't resist. That Sylvia Kristel, she did it for me. *If only.* Okay, she didn't have much in the chest department but she had the tidiest arse I'd ever seen on a woman (or man come to think of it, which I never did) and what a mouth she possessed, almost inviting you to... well, you get the picture.

'Hi, you look great,' I said, planting a kiss on Paula's cheek. *'Come in, I'll put that in the fridge, it still works even though Dibble peed on it the other week.'*

'You're joking?' she said with that lovely, gentle yet lively Mersey accent.

'Yeah I am. It was the video recorder. It still works an' all! Er... not that I hardly use it, course.'

'I do love your accent Steve, it's so... so rough but warm,' she said. I'd never really thought about it before, that I even had an accent.

'Is thy tekking piss out of mi accent, lass? I like yours too Liver bird!'

* * *

A problem dawned on me - more like 'dusked' really - one which I'd not prepared for at all. Should I invite her in to my room straight away - where my bed, hifi and black & white TV were - or in to the communal lounge with comfier furniture, colour television and video? If I succeeded in luring her in to my bedroom too early then there was every chance I'd have little chance of getting the chance to chance my arm for a slice. And then again, if I dawdled too long in the lounge then I just knew I'd bottle out of asking her to enter my parlour. Also, to be blunt and with no disrespect, there was little chance of *her* asking to go in.

I'd heard of but never actually understood the warnings of mixing 'grain with grape'. It was Ian, unsurprisingly, who informed me one day what it meant. No major surprise there like I said, he seemed to know everything did Ian. That was outstanding office leadership and interpersonal skills for you. Alas, his advice came too late for me and Paula. The wine Paula had brought, plus a sneaky red from my room, combined with a fair few lagers meant we were both well tanked up. The lager and wine quickly had me well drunk but in a delayed reaction sort of way, like I wasn't properly aware it was happening. So, even though I knew I was (un)steadily on my way, I was quite convinced I could handle it and wasn't in too bad a state. But I *was* man, man was I. And, with no chauvinism intended, girls can't take their drink as well as boys. We sat in the lounge drinking, talking, watching bilge on TV. And as the drink took hold of us, we took hold of each other and I was swimming in drink and happiness. We ended up in my room, on my bed, listening to records. I had no idea how we'd got there, besides by staggering obviously, or which magic words of persuasion, *begging* maybe, I'd enchanted her with, or even what time it was.

No matter, this was all now getting horny. Horni**er** to be exact. Somehow, and God did I thank God for the state of affairs, I was lying on my back on the bed with her straddling me. And with The Stranglers' *La Folie* album playing too, this was near bliss! We were fully clothed but it didn't call for much imagination for certain messages to get across. Practically sitting on me, I was completely under her control, she was in command of the proceedings. Lavish, absolutely lavish. And proceed, we did just that. This was a new Paula, a passionate, thirsty, desiring Paula, and I was loving her dominating matters. She kissed, nibbled, licked, *bit* my face and neck. Her tongue explored my mouth, her hands stroked, probed, *gripped* my body. All I wanted now was for her to search more and find out what I had for her below waist.

As she continued to kiss me passionately - I could taste blood, our lips and teeth had impacted so much - I slipped my hands up her hot back and expertly unclasped her bra strap. Neither flinching or faltering, she was giving wonderful vibes and I was pulse-pumpingly thrilled. I stroked and caressed her ribs as she plunged her tongue further in to my mouth, and then I reached the early stages of my Holy Grail, cupping, fondling her wonderful, firm breasts. She gasped as I tweaked her nipples and pinched her tongue with my teeth, she was loving it, loving every single second of it. I could scent her desire, that delightful sharp almost spicy aroma. I wanted to taste it, and was hopeful I'd get the chance, I'd never done that before. Breathing hard, her tongue thrashing around in my mouth and her lips pressing hard, grinding, she dragged her top off. Although it was dark, I could see the silhouette of my gorgeous girl as she flung her top to the floor and shook her hair alluringly, preparing to dive back on to, in to, me.

Staring hard in the dark, wide-eyed I gazed into her face. I didn't see Paula, I saw the glorious, perfect visage and stunning eyes, of Grace Kelly. Yes, Grace Kelly, *that* Grace Kelly. Grace Kelly of *Rear Window* and *Dial M for Murder.* My second love had always been Shirley Eaton in *Goldfinger*, they were the two most beautiful women I'd ever seen. And here was I, about to make love with one of these perfect women. It didn't matter whether I was drunk, sober or insane, it was **really** happening, the moment could never be taken away from me. Grace Kelly was writhing on top of me, wanting me. She was hot, she was needful and she was wearing only knickers, rubbing herself against my manhood. This was better than any film. This was better than any **dream**.

But then she paused.
Oh no, please God no pausing, don't let her lose her nerve. Please no...

No, she was readying herself for the final plunge, the leap to womanhood, and I was convinced, at that very moment, that Paula was **the** girl for me. I wanted to be with her forever, my heart was throbbing, racing everywhere. We'd marry young, have kids, grow old together and be with each other for life. She grappled with my belt and slowly, slowly dragged my zip down. It seemed to take a lifetime. I didn't want to say anything, I didn't want to distract her, to disturb her. Raising herself off the bed she slowly peeled her knickers off, leaving me hovering. Over the music, I thought I heard a bump outside. I didn't care, as long as she didn't stop. She dispensed with her panties to the floor. I couldn't think of anything on earth sexier than a girl taking off her underwear, preparing to give herself to me.
And then she whispered, a slurred, *'Have you any contraceptives?'*

Yes I did. I reached to the side of my bed for the dresser top drawer. One of my favourite tracks, *Everybody Loves You When You're Dead* came on as I managed to grasp a Durex packet.

'*Can I* do it?' she asked.

Could she?! This angel was fast making my night heavenly euphoric. God, I wanted, needed to thrust myself into her soon, to grind and penetrate; to nail, to *make* her. We would soon be there, oh yes, as one. Come on! I'd been needing this moment for ages; it was vital for our relationship too. These were the essentials of life, the moments you yearn for while knowing also that you're absolutely loving the wait and the anticipation. The elixir of life wasn't drinking, football or music, it was moments like these, being with someone you've been pining for and finally reaching, about to unite with them.

THUD THUD THUD on my bedroom door. And then '*I hope you're not shagging in there, Steve!'* came Dibble's raucous voice. I was startled. Paula wasn't so much startled but scared, **terrified.** Terrified and with a cry of shock, she toppled off the bed on to the floor - and out of my life - with a painful, excruciating, humiliating bump.

* * *

13   Dirty Laundry

You still didn't have to hit him,' Ian preached.

'Shit, course I did! What would you have done?'

'I wouldn't have hit him.'

'You're totally out of order,' chipped in Dodds.

They weren't listening to me, they weren't understanding me. They were on a different bloody planet and totally out of order having a dig at me.

'Don't you start!' I shouted. *'That bastard has just ruined me and Paula!'*

Dodds snorted. *'You were only trying to get your end away with another bird.'*

'No matter what, friends don't hit friends, it's just wrong Steve, plain and simple,' said Ian.

I left the living room. *'Go bollocks, the lot of yer!'*

Who were they to preach? I'd done nothing wrong and look at the crap I had to deal with now, thanks to that big-mouthed runt. Before, the three of them had each brought girls back just for one thing and then tossed them aside like used teabags. We'd all been guilty of that but now I was trying to change. Dodds once even had a threesome and had invited Dibble to help him out. Now *they* were slagging *me*!

I went back in, I had to say something, anything, to show them how I felt. I was the one hard done to, not Dibble, no way. Still drunk though, I couldn't be sure what it was I needed to tell them, that was the problem. I stood in the doorway for a few seconds, gathering my thoughts, trying to focus better.

'Look,' I near shouted, *'I'm still half pissed but I have to say this.'*

'Get stuffed,' came back at me.

'Shut it, Dodds, hear me out will yer.' I barked. He stayed quiet.

'Alright,' I said, *'I admit I shouldn't have hit Dibble but he wound me up that much, I snapped. He's always doing it, you two know it as well as I do...'*

Ian was about to interrupt but I carried on. *'I'll apologise in t'morning, I swear.'*

I gulped as the next part suddenly sprang into my mind. I knew it would be hard saying it but I had to get it out - *'Lads, you're just about the best mates I've got. And I even thought me and Dibble were getting on more than okay...'* I took a deep breath, if I wasn't careful I'd be getting far too emotional for my own good. We were all drunk though... *'You know how hard life's been for me. I'm not complaining but I mean it, you lot have helped me. And so has Paula, she was important to me.'*

'Alright Steve, calm down and get yourself to bed. We've all had our moments in this house, Dibble prob'ly more than anyone.' Ian reasoned. *'Let's sort it out tomorrow.'*

Dibble had been lucky I didn't hit him more than the once, and it wasn't so hard a punch in any case, probably hurting my knuckles more than his jaw. I did apologise though, but I wasn't sure whether Dibble and me could ever be quite the same again. I'd hurt him physically but he'd hurt me more, whether or not it was intended. More painfully, as time passed and as the night's events never quite faded from my memory, me and Paula were never *anything* again.

14   Seasons in the Sun, and Other Gutter Rags

Leeds United were, as I often muttered to myself, garbage, and consistently mediocre for way too long to be anything but perennial second-rate Second Division disappointers. It hurt to admit it, especially as fans continually forked out more money than was decent to watch them across the country. The 1982/83 season, the start of a new life for Leeds, had held all sorts of exciting promise and potential but ultimately we were let down. Again. I was never too sure whether the Board sacking Allan Clarke before the start of that new season was a good idea. He was at least one thing: a proud man and he loved Leeds United. During his playing career he'd lived Leeds United too, that's why the fans loved him. He was a winner as a player, no way would he just accept being a loser as a manager. But players failed him and it shouldn't be forgotten the team had precious little good luck that season.

After the dismissal of Clarkey, in came everyone's favourite Leeds 'son': Eddie Gray. Wonderful player and regarded as an ambassador for football, the choosing of Eddie would keep the fans happy and maybe even help sort the club out. So we dreamed anyway, but the thing was, and it wasn't hard to see if you looked hard enough, the Board gave him the job because he was a cheap and hopeful option. Reading that another way, Eddie Gray had been given an unwanted pup and bugger all funds to feed it with. For him to guide Leeds back to Division One would have been a miracle, and miracles rarely happened, not in football anyway and certainly not with Leeds United. His first season in charge was respectable if unspectacular, and we finished ninth in Division Two. Attendances at Elland Road, despite the team having a good home record, dipped alarmingly again. The support for away games was a different story.

I can't state categorically but I'm sure the number of travelling fans actually increased. Unfortunately for the club and for Eddie, trouble was never far away from Leeds fans and battles and riots were commonplace. I loved it and I hated it - with the exception of obscene chanting to goad opposing supporters I never properly got involved in the violence, I wasn't brave enough. That was the truth though I do excuse myself with the desire of not adding to my criminal record. If I'd got involved, knowing my luck I'd have been plucked out of the crowd by some over-zealous zealot of a policeman for *thinking* derogatory thoughts. I did understand why trouble happened at matches and what a high buzz it gave the participants, fighting enemy fans and trashing their towns. On the other hand, of course, knifing, glassing and slashing people was seriously wrong. Always will be naturally, and whilst you didn't hear of it happening at Leeds games so much, there was always rumour that a favourite 'work tool' of the Service Crew was the good old Stanley knife. Hooliganism was happening everywhere, in every division and probably in every footballing country, too. British fans were getting banned left, right and centre and the government was forever blaming the clubs. And they had their favourite targets as well. Violence at football was forever in the tabloids, even one gang of Leeds fans featured in a national Sunday paper/Monday fish and chip wrapper.

Blimey, I can't half harp on about Leeds United when I get going. So here's more...

What the government and FA did wasn't right but I suppose they'd run out of ideas on how to control all the violence on the terraces and around football grounds. Leeds were playing at home to QPR in 1982 in Division Two. Due to more Leeds fan shenanigans the FA had closed down half of Elland Road stadium for a couple of matches. This was one of those matches and we were up against a good Rangers team led by the alleged tactical genius Terry Venables. Watching from my new, temporary seat in the South Stand, I wished I hadn't bothered, I hated sitting at games for one thing. Plus 'tactical genius' Venables my uncomfortably numb behind, his team played the offside trap all day long. Well it felt like a day at least. Leeds lost 1-0 and I swear I was never so bored in my whole spectating life at watching such drivel. Even worse than watching an England friendly. No, seriously. We had fun going to Leeds' away games though, it always made up for the often meagre fare. The 'banned' trips were even better (it isn't possible to ban Leeds fans) as opposing fans were almost on our side against the FA. I loved *all* the trips with the Fullerton, they looked after you as well as viewing visits to at least one new pub before a match as essential.

The next season was, on paper, worse - Leeds finished tenth, a less than respectable position on the face of it. But most of the fans had woken to the fact that Eddie had a virtually impossible job to do trying to rebuild the club; and were patient about it. Leeds got well and truly tonked away from home at such fortresses as Shrewsbury and Oxford but Eddie was making progress with new exciting young players together with the return of 'past masters' like Lorimer, David Harvey and Eddie's younger brother Frank Gray. Even Peter Barnes came back for a short stint. There promised to be exciting times, some of these 'young uns' looked good potential. I couldn't speak for everyone obviously but with Eddie Gray in charge I doubt any reasonably minded supporter thought he was doing a bad job or that he should be sacked.

October 1985 and it was all over the papers, even the front headlines of the Evening Post: a photo of a smart looking young man sitting, slouching near enough, in an office chair looking like he'd lost everything he'd ever loved. That dejected gentleman was Eddie Gray, the Board had finished him after a pretty gloomy first few months of a new season. True, Leeds had lost at Stoke 6-2 (our coach broke down and we still caught fifteen minutes play and two Stoke goals) and there were poor defeats to Fulham, Huddersfield and Carlisle but you shouldn't sack a young manager with a young team in a season only three months old. Yes, three months. The treatment of Eddie Gray was little short of disgraceful. We were just about used to such shoddy crap though, not much was surprising anymore where Elland Road was concerned. The day of Eddie's departure, one of the lads rang me at work to tell me it had happened. Eric, my boss and very well informed Leeds sage, refused to believe me. I never did ask him: why would I lie about it? I'm not embarrassed to admit it - well, I am a bit - I had tears in my eyes for Eddie. I wasn't alone, many were appalled and there were even rumours the players, led by Lorimer, were threatening to go on strike. I'm glad they didn't, we'd had enough doomed industrial disputes in the North without our footie team joining in. It was somehow gratifying to see that the players did care though.

Life went on regardless of how strongly or passionately I felt about the dire matters of Leeds United - I had absolutely no influence on what would happen there, I was only a young oik of a supporter who went to most but not even all the matches. So I was irrelevant, the club cared not a jot about me or others like me. In truth it didn't pain me to think like that, I recognised I had a lowly standing, I was fortunate enough to be able to be quite mature about it all. And by those methods, the pain of events subsided quite quickly, it never got *too much* to bear any more. After all, nothing could be as bad as the European Cup Final or an FA Cup Semi Final defeat to Scum or the horror of West Bromwich in '82. And course, I had my own football team to care about, as well as my social life with the lads and trying to resurrect a practically dead love life. So, when they announced who the new manager was to replace Edwin Gray Esquire, I had a sense of fresh optimism. Life, as I said, went on and Eddie Gray would live and no doubt come back stronger. The appointment of Billy Bremner as his successor was, I thought, a possible brainwave (at last) by the Board.

If anyone had the power and influence to really get the players motivated enough to shed blood and win glory again for the LUFC cause then surely it was he.

15   Chase

> *'Beeston Whites, we are here,*
> *Shag your women and drink your beer!'*

All just a bit of fun between Leeds fans from various areas of the city. *'Insert your district name here'*. Mind you, it could never be always harmonious on the Kop. Billy Bremner taking over from Eddie had seen improvements but there were still disgruntled supporters upset about the Board's treatment of Gray and overall, the results remained remarkably familiar: poor. Leeds finished fourteenth in '85/'86. It wasn't all doom and gloom though, we still had hope on the terraces and players like Sheridan, Aspin, Baird, Ritchie and new signings like Ormsby, Edwards, Adams, Rennie and Pearson gave some, if not massive, reason for optimism. Billy's team actually managed to go one better than Eddie's the week before this particular Boxing Day match. Away at Stoke, Leeds had lost 7-2 (seven). Blooming hell, and just before Christmas too, cheers lads - Season's bleeding Greetings to you too!

If I went to games on my own I'd stand near the front right of the Kop but if I was with one of the lads we'd stand in the middle for the rough and tumble. Anything to get my mind off Paula, that's how I viewed it and how I should have, as a sensible young man. Sensible was never something you'd immediately associate with me though: I shocked myself at how often I still let her enter my mind. I mean, it had been *ages* ago, I was a right maudlin sap when I 'wanted' to be. No doubt, by then, she'll have been back in Liverpool and blissfully in love with some student or some scally, and deep down I knew it was right we never got back together again. Supporting my football team was a decent distraction from such daftness. So was beer obviously, except the memory loss caused by ale resulted in *double* loneliness as I trudged towards being sober the morning after. *Sobriety was the vice of life*, for me anyway, if 'life' was what you could call my presence on the planet at the time. With a hangover I was pathetic, truly pathetic. Whenever I thought of her, my heart really would flinch and miss a beat. It was too easy to say 'Don't think of her', I wish I could have stopped. The first cut is the deepest and all that, and it was right. I drank to get drunk and to get over the wound, seeking relief and forgetting that the return from drink to normality increased the solitude and depression. Those are times when friends can really prove their worth - but for them to be able to do so you have to open up and confide.

My love life should have been sued under the Trade Descriptions Act, as it wasn't actually alive at all. Girls I really did fancy would already be attached and any I finally did manage to go out with were using me as a *possible* replacement for their present partners, to see if I was a better alternative. Two I recall, in one year, who married the fellas within three months of throwing me away like a half-eaten apple. Maybe I looked confident and capable of taking the knocks but actually it damaged me, I took it all to heart, no doubt too much but that's so easy when you're already down. Never had I *deliberately* hurt anyone, but I had hurt some in the past, it was unavoidable, and I started to believe I was paying Life back for such bad behaviour. Could I do anything about it, about being this melancholy self-pitying sap? No; I was too weak to consider stopping drinking, ignoring the fact that the higher alcohol took me, the heavier the falls got. Being a saddo single also-ran at Christmas and sodding Valentines especially rammed home the feeling it really was sin payback time. I tell you, the pocket of my heart suffered the debt badly.

* * *

I was born a Beeston White. Well, Leeds General Infirmary White to be precise, but you get the meaning. On match days, usually before kick off or half time, you could hear any number of united Leeds districts - and areas in and away from West Yorkshire - singing their own version of the 'Women and Beer' song. There was the occasional jostle and full-blown scrapping but it was usually peaceful noise, if you see my point. You'd hear singing Whites from Miggy, Belle Isle, Bramley, Seacroft, Pontefract (Ponte Carlo and Cas Vegas), Kippax (of course), Rothwell, and so on and on. I picked up a few lost badges over the Gelderd years too, like a very basic designed 70's one with 'Fev Whites' hand-written on it, and a crudely etched 'Tony Currie Shoots Faster than a Sex Pistol!' one. I loved Tony Currie, he was brilliant, always better than Glenn Hoddle. That was from 1977 days though, we were nearly a decade on now. Like lost loves, I should have stopped myself looking back at the Currie days. Back to those badges: you could pick fault with the artistry but not the sentiment, which said much about the camaraderie and unity of Leeds supporters most of the time, home and away. Some faces you wouldn't wish to associate with - or even look at to be brutally honest, unless you were looking to be brutalised - but 'family' was what these Loiners (natural or adopted) stood for. We were all on the same side.

Old Lane, Beeston; it joined the bottom of Middleton Hill ('Miggy' Hill to friends) and stretched all the way across to the Beeston Co-op and St Mary's Church and graveyard. Old Lane was always an appealing road, the houses generally were large and attractive and most gardens had a satisfying prettiness about them. To me, Old Lane ran through the district of Beeston like a sturdy spine spanning an impressive frame. Daft really but what the hell, I sometimes felt poetic. Or pathetic, judging by my dodgy poetry. The post office was there for ever it seemed, and next door was the House of Pain (the dentist's) and a few yards further on the doctor's surgery where I think I had a season ticket I visited that much as a nipper. The dentist visits usually *were* painful but it was always a pleasure seeing my dentist Mr Parr. He had to stoop to enter the room, I swear, this tall silver-haired bespectacled chap with a deep but gentle voice. He seemed a really good bloke, despite the trauma he often inflicted on me and my mouth. It was there where I got a front tooth capped after being headbutted by a certain nazi slug, and that was bloody agony. I remember getting home after Mr Parr had done his work - with my gum throbbing like a bass drum - and finding splashes of blood, *on my forehead*.

The back gardens of those semi-detached houses running opposite Moorhouse's jam factory (before it got toasted) were absolutely brilliant for Beeston's major steeplechase race. Most people never even knew Beeston had a racecourse, I tell you; who'd believe that? Somehow, even though those gardens were only a few yards away from my Elmhurst abode, I myself never managed to participate in the LS11 Grand National. In fact, I never even saw it happen, it was spoken of in almost mythical awe. Maybe I was always too busy with *Kick Out Ball*, hedge diving or plain old *One, Two, Three*, I don't know, or even *Star Trek* on the box, but I was forever jealous for missing out. Because there was never any deliberate damage incurred on Old Lane residents' property - so they said anyway - I think the Grand National runners would escape any legal proceedings if they were named. Just as well really, because they're about to be. As far as I was told, virtually every teenaged lad who knocked about the area took part in the National. So lads from various South Leeds families were involved, like the Grimshaws, and the Carters, Campbells, Browns, Parkers, Metcalfs, Gomersalls, Kitchensons, the Inneses, the Crosslands, Devlins, Hatfields, Hickinsons, Briggs, Biggsy, Pass's, the Hurleys and Tyrers; the list seemed endless. It was definitely Bottomley-less anybloomingway.

I would never have won anyhow, I was slow, couldn't climb well and was garbage at hurdling; I'd've been an also (nearly) ran. I would have loved to see the time, when one lawn, gloriously illuminated by the light coming from behind French windows, played host to seven or eight lads dancing the Can Can. They carried on Can Canning for ages, completely unnoticed by the oblivious telly-watching residents.

* * *

Sunderland fans, the Plastic Geordies as unkinder sorts called them (me being one of them) were famous for their passionate and loyal support. Allegedly. It was irrefutably 'allegedly' when considering their low home attendances. Strange loyalty that, and we'd seen enough of such loyalty ourselves to know. I was deliberately unfair on Sunderland, due to them beating Leeds in the FA Cup Final of '73. They played well and deserved to win but that didn't lessen the bitterness of us losing yet another important game. Everyone remembers their goalkeeper Jim Montgomery having a blinder, one double-save in particular; and yes, he was superb. That brace of saves, first a diving header from Trevor Cherry and then a Lorimer lash - were the most memorable. I cursed every time I saw the clip, and the BBC loved to show it regularly, very regularly. In fact, it got that bad they started showing a weekly programme called 'Sunderland Humiliating Leeds United'. Actually, I cursed *Cherry* every time I saw it, not Montgomery. If you watch Cherry, after his header, if he'd get to his feet straight away instead of lying around like a beached seal, he has a clear net to tap the ball into as Lorimer's parried shot rolls right next to him. All he does though is flap a shin like it's a weak and feeble fin at it.

By now, back home at my Mum's as it was easier for me to get to work, it meant saving money was easier and I was closer to Elland Road. The Headingley boys hadn't been exactly chuffed with me leaving but were okay about it. It meant they'd have to pay a bit more rent or get someone else in, that was all. They never did though, funnily enough, and so I often kipped up there after nights out. This particular day, I watched the Leeds-Sunderland game with Bruges but we'd got separated in the dark afterwards on Lowfields Road. Some trouble kicked off even though there was only twenty-one thousand at the game (a boring one all draw - *and* our goal was an o.g.). As one Leeds fan in his twenties ran by me - fleeing - to the rear of the Kop end, *away* from Sunderland fans, shouting with no shame or irony whatsoever, *'Come on, they're only Sunderland!'* At that moment I should have sussed things might not turn out too well.

Annoyed at Leeds' performance - and wondering how much more second rate Division Two life we'd have to stomach - I actually was quite up for watching Leeds lads get the Sunderland fans and to support them (vocally) nearby. It was chaos all over the Lowfields Road - the police in their wisdom had let the away fans out while there were still dozens of Leeds lads loitering with intent, in small and not so small strategically positioned groups. Ten or so horse-back officers tried to disperse waiting Leeds gangs but only really succeeded in flattening and terrifying innocent people trying to get home. At the same time, about fifty on-foot policemen attempted to form a human barrier around the away fans in the direction of the town centre. It was like trying to embrace fog: men were easily evading the confines; it was daft. And virtually all the supporters were without club colours. The threat of a punch up with an oppos-

ing mob was frightening enough but not knowing which mob was which made it worse. It could be an addictive tingle though, could fear. Individual Leeds fans freely waded in to the column of Sunderland fans, lamping anyone in the vicinity, while Sunderland fans splintered away to regroup and have a go back. It was fascinating viewing from the wall I was standing on with a few others, in safety. Under the dazzling floodlights though, as the crowds slowly dwindled, so did the action. I decided to depart, making sure the odd stray Sunderland dog wasn't slyly targeting me. I zipped my Harrington up to my throat to keep warm-ish and to conceal my yellow Leeds scarf. Small pockets of Leeds fans loitered near the foot of Wesley Street, still searching for trouble. Officers persisted in trying to move them on, it was still like trying to sweep leaves in a gale, only these leaves were cocky and verbally abusive with it. Naturally such behaviour riled the coppers: one suddenly suspected me of giving him lip. He challenged me, *'What did you just say?'*
'I didn't say owt!' I protested, trying to sound innocent, tough and resentful all at the same time. A difficult combination that.
'Get home then,' he ordered, shoving me in the back. I didn't deserve the extra touch, there was no call for it.
I kept quiet but I was narked, I'd been wronged yet again, and by the law again. I wanted, needed, to take it out on something, someone, and I wasn't prepared to go up to my Headingley former-home to kick a certain cat.

Obviously, I couldn't do anything against a Bobby even if he'd asked for it (which, let's get it right, he just about had done). Soon after, as I approached the top of the Wesley Street hill, I spotted a small bloke in a shiny black coat and red and white scarf around his neck, slipping round the corner to the car park between the Co-op and the White Hart. I was confused: I knew it was wrong but I wanted him slapped. I wasn't so bad though, it wouldn't be me doing the hurting. A shout of *'Get the ponce'* (in a definite non-Yorkshire accent) snapped me to reality anyway. Immediately a group of six or seven lads raced after the Sunderland fan. This might be fun I thought, and I ran after them. Slipping between crawling traffic I reached the well-lit car park and saw the lads hurtle over the far wall in pursuit. They entered the darkness of the muck track between the Old Lane back gardens and the King Field allotments.

The trail was near completely pitch black so it was quite a brave route to take on any night; not recommended for faint heart, that's for sure. Funnily enough, looking back on that track you'd be dazzled by the far away floodlights yet in front of you was like a void of sheer black. Into the charcoal mouth I dived, I was fascinated. I couldn't see our lads but I could hear them shouting. The ground there always was treacherous, and tonight it was rock hard with the cold so I didn't run, I just tried to walk quickly in the darkness. I'd soon lost them all. I calmed down, I'd come to my senses and was looking forward to a nice cup of cocoa and maybe a turkey sandwich, in front of the fire. Then someone had me in a headlock.

'Yer not after me lad, are yer?' It was the Sunderland fan, and the question more a challenge than enquiry.

'No, no, I'm just on mi way 'ome,' I said, and it was the truth, albeit not exactly the whole truth.

'Good job, else I'd've battered yer.' And then he grabbed at my scarf, scratching my chin as he did so, the cheeky bastard. The material burned the nape of my neck too. He probably *could* have battered me but he wasn't having my colours, no way; it cost me two quid and I was cold. *'These colours don't run'*, what a cracking quote, wish I'd used it. I tore free, snatching my scarf back.

'Get off me you plastic Geordie shithead!' too. I bet he felt like burying himself in the ground I'd hurt him so much with my vitriol, I don't think. I was nearly sure he didn't chase after me but I kept on running just in case, like you do, out of the dark and in to the haven of the orange light of Old Lane. Even better, I emerged to see the Leeds fellas walking towards me.

But *'What yer running for?'* sneered one. I didn't like his tone but fair enough, emotions were high and mistaken identity was obviously possible.

'Just found that Sunderland bloke, hiding in...'

'And you ran away?' snorted another deeper voice. I still couldn't grasp their accents.

'Bastard coward,' grunted another. I laughed for a second, stupidly thinking he meant the Sunderland bloke then realised he meant me. Now I didn't care where they were from, I just wished they weren't there where I was. They were Leeds fans true, but not of the Leeds *community,* and worse, for some unstated reason they were after me.

'I'm a Leeds fan!' I shouted as I darted across Old Lane in to the

Jessamine streets. I should have gone to the right, towards our house: my Mum would have sorted them out, no danger.

There was hardly any traffic. They set off after me but I had a good start. I possibly ran my quickest ever and was easily beating them (I never beat anyone). The threat wasn't over though, they were still after me. I nipped past St Anthony's School, wishing I was fitter as my pained lungs and throat protested coldly. In to the first back street of big terraced houses I ran. I'd have enough breathing space to finally dodge them but just to be on the safe side I hid in a small dark backyard about three houses down, surrounded by.plant pots and tall garden tools. I crouched behind a metal dustbin, safe and sound as a hound in a pound. Relief washed over me, I'd had a lucky escape, though admittedly it wasn't exactly luck I felt in having to flee from fellow fans.

Soon I heard voices, low, conspiring, about to give up the chase they said, suspecting, rightly, that they'd lost me. I was in the clear, I'd got away and in one more minute I'd be securely sneaking home. I almost chuckled. Then a friendly young white cat appeared, angling and mewing for my attention. I gave it some, introducing it to the back of my hand and swiping it away, right under the eyes of three of my pursuers watching over the wall. That little sod had let my cat out of the bag. As soon as they saw me they pounced, storming in through the gate - near flooring each other in desperation to get at me.
'I'm a Leeds fan, lads!' I whined again, quickly standing. No reply.

It didn't matter who or what I was, they landed punches and kicks all over my head and torso, I managed to swipe blows away before covering my head with my arms. What strikes did impact I didn't really feel, that's the truth, my shaking with panic numbed them. I crouched to my haunches, keeping my head protected as the fists kept pounding. Not one brave strike hurt; I hurt myself more, inside, cursing myself, cursing cursing, wishing I'd stand up to them, wishing I could defend myself. Deep down I knew I could and I was sure I could have taken one of them, but I was petrified, I really couldn't move. The assault ceased and the bastards retreated. I managed to stand, only to then collapse and slide back down the wall, my trembling legs outstretched on the ground. My arms shivered, I was defeated, miserable and spent. With my eyes closed, bitter stinging tears formed and flowed as I started to sob. I heard my new found enemies walk away down the street.

'Got him!' one celebrated, the sick shit. Then I heard a scamper of feet. I looked up to see another one enter the garden. Watching him, almost hopeful, I thought maybe he wanted to apologise or to even try and help me. In a way I wasn't disappointed, as he did say *'Sorry mate'*, following up with *'You shouldn't've run away'* as he crashed the spikes of a garden rake down on to my left ankle.

Those brave lads, especially that one, scarred me for life.

16   Slappers

The police told me there was virtually no chance they'd catch the pricks who battered me. I just wanted to forget about it all but one of the residents had rung the police so it meant a Crime Report had to be completed, for the record and all that rubbish. I was proud for not blubbing when recounting the events to the two coppers.

Weeks later and it was history. And just like History at school it became practically erased from my mind. Okay, I was a bit edgier for a while but nothing massive. Anyway, *'In Shreds'* by The Chameleons snapped me in to consciousness this Sunday morning. The pumping, aggressive, *dirty* song got me thinking, about sex. Not much change there it might be noted, me thinking of sex on a morning. But this was slightly different.

'Sunday morning'... and I felt like whoring. Yes, really, I was up for it, tired of not having a girlfriend and bored with servicing myself. Me and Dodds had been talking about it one night, though he was only half serious about doing it, that was quite clear. And then Dibble joined in, goading me and calling me a coward, saying I'd never have the nerve. But for me things had got so bad even my right hand was blanking me. Out with the lads I hardly got the slightest of interested glances from women any more. Or if I did, I bloody missed them. Maybe I was looking too hard, maybe I looked desperate.

In the end, it was one of those ideas which, on second thoughts, I wished had come at least third in my reckoning. Then again, I'd compiled a league table of self-inflicted regrets in my love life, one more couldn't make much difference. I was going without the favourite fix of female company and it was killing me. Not bleeding softly either. I'd suffered for too long, not so much from *coitus interruptus* but *coitus intabouttohappen(ever)*. During my time with Paula, Paula who for so long withheld privileges from me until that one doomed night, I was a one woman man. Technically I suppose one woman *half* man, seeing as I didn't get what a whole man should from a relationship.

* * *

I'd kipped at the lads' gaffe in Headingley Avenue for a few days, much to the annoyance of my own personal hotelier, my mother. I must have been mental, it was winter and the landlord was still a total git. For every night I stayed there, I paid the lads in Skyrack beer.

'Come on then, let's do it. If you're absolutely sure, Steve?' asked Ian sensibly, inserting the ignition key.

'I'm sure mate,' I replied. *'I'm sure.'* I was confident this little adventure would go no further than we four: I'd made them swear secrecy.

'Have you still got a Cash and Carry card?' chipped in Dibble.

'Are you taking the piss?' he was, why I even asked I don't know.

'You never know, you might get a discount for gash!'

'You dirty bastard, Dibble,' piped up Dodds.

*'**Me** the dirty bastard?'*

'Dibble, stay at home if you're not gonna take this seriously,' added Ian, seriously. *'I don't want to get in to any bother due to your crater mouth.'*

'Alright, I'm sorry. You big pansies.'

There I was, about to do something quite brave and dangerous and all Dibble could do was try to make a joke of it all. Sometimes I was glad I'd hit him - *'Dibble, you are one piece of shit, I can't believe you and me have ever been mates.'*

He stayed quiet. Result.

Well, at least until *'Tosser'* arrived in the guise of a cough.

The four of us in the Vauxhall Viva we all generally hated but had all generally taken advantage of over the years, turned off at the bottom of Headingley Avenue towards an area of suburban Leeds: Chapeltown. The roads were very quiet, it was a Sunday night and Sunday nights were never worth much in any capacity except being the night before the start of the next rotten week, with people staying in or going to bed early, hoping to delay or switch off from the inevitable. When we die, which despite Mr Grim Reaper usually not being *invited*, we all will do, it should be on a Sunday as sod all ever happens on them. It was past eleven, yet *strangely*, the lads wanted to join me and Ian despite usually going to bed early on Sundays.

Spencer Place in Chapeltown was the most famous - infamous, let's get it right - red light area of Leeds. Oddly though, it almost looked salubrious an area to me, and that was nothing to do with coming from Beeston. We'd pass through there on Sunday mornings on our way to Soldier's Field for the odd Flatts game. It was a long street of big old houses with long gardens and huge, healthy trees on the pavement. Some of the houses were a bit dishevelled yes, but they and the grounds they stood on must have been worth a fortune. Come nightfall however, the apparent serenity of daytime became masked in darkness and shadows, as values dropped and shady characters scuttled around. High heeled, short-skirted ladies would emerge, alone or in twos or threes, offering their wares and their services to interested individuals. Any sympathies I had for the *normal* local residents disintegrated as I stooped to be one of those interested takers on this night. And I didn't feel ashamed, I was focused on having my way with a new woman, a new conquest: fresh meat.

Which came first, the prostitute or the dreg wanting to have her? And how soon after crawled the pimp from his particular pit? I should stress that these questions only occurred to me afterwards. Before and during, well, there was only one thing on my mind, and that was to shoot into a woman. No questions asked, no consequences, that was the plan and at a cost of less than a night out on the ale.

I didn't have butterflies in my stomach no, they felt more like albatrosses. I wasn't just nervous about being a first timer with a prostitute, I was nervous about who was out there with them, who would know what I was up to and who was looking after these women, what threat they were to me. And maybe the police would be sniffing around as well, watching, monitoring, lurking to pounce on low life kerb crawlers like me. Worse, what if it was the lads who got nicked? That would have been funny actually, even though they'd have been after my blood as a result. Nonetheless, with all these worries preying on my mind and the flutters in my gut, I still was intent on going through with it.

'There's one!' Dodds pointed out from the backseat behind me, like he was on a safari. *'What d'you reckon, Steve? She good enough for you?'*

'Give us a break Dodds, I've only just clocked her.'

'Cocked her?' chirped Dibble.

Ian rolled the car up to the kerb and parked, keeping the Viva engine purring like a cat. With asthma. Leaning against a grubby white garden wall was a lone girl, about twenty-five, with dark curly hair, short black leather skirt, podgy white legs under gaping fishnets, wearing white high heels.

'Well? She the one? I don't want to hang around, I'm a bit nervous' said Ian, nervously.

'Why? No one's gonna nick this shit heap,' enquired Dibble.

'Get out if you don't like it, you tosser,' Ian snapped, snappily.

'Yeah, let's do it - been with worse,' I blurted as I wound the window down.

'No argument there,' added Dibble.

The woman stepped towards us, coolly, near disinterestedly.

'Hi, I'm Antoinette. Want some fun?' she asked through a chewful of gum, not completely convincing me she'd be able to provide it. I heard Dibble smirk in the back seat.

*'You could **marry** Antoinette, Steve!'* he sniggered. Quite clever for him that.

'Yeah, how much?' I asked her.

I couldn't believe I was there, never mind talking business with a Princess of the Streets.

She looked in to the back seat, then down and up the street, checking.

'We're not coppers love!' declared Dibble.

'Alright!' she sniped, *'A tenner for straight sex, more for extras.'*

'That'll do, ta,' I said. And then she gave Dodds a fright, knocking on his window.

'Budge up then, blondie.'

I got out of the front passenger seat - she then decided it would be better for me to get in the back; so I did; and then I got a bit confused.

'We gonna do it here?' I asked. Everyone laughed at me, even Ian though more politely. It lifted the tension - for them at least.

She spoke to Ian. I didn't listen to her directions but judging by the very short time it took to get there, her 'work place' wasn't far from Spencer Place. Not one more word was spoken during the journey - by then I was bricking it, the last thing on my mind was to speak. I didn't have a clue on what the decorum of pre-paid-for sex on a cold Sunday night in a dark and seedy part of my hometown was anyway.

'Here'll do,' she told him. He parked outside a small dodgy looking terraced house with a front garden of uneven paving slabs, broken fence and wonky gate. Apparently, we'd arrived. She turned around to me, *'Is it just you then, big boy?'* What a question, the filthy cow, it even wiped the grin off Dibble's face.

I replied, kind of, *'Er...'.* She got out of the car and adeptly pulled the seat forward for me to leave with her. She took my hand and we walked down the short garden path to the dirty, peeling door.

I accidentally bumped the gate, it clattered on the ground.

*'At least **you're** a real man,'* she said, unlocking the door. She didn't sound like she meant it.

It was dark and the floors and stairs were bare and no working light. The walls were stripped and cold, clammy. She shone a torch to lead me to the bedroom. As I entered I looked back at the door opposite, across the landing. It creaked as it drifted ajar. I couldn't be sure but I sensed I was being watched and being *informed* that someone else was present in that desolate place. In Antoinette's room, no electric light, she lit a solitary candle standing in a saucer on a white bedside table.

'Get undressed then,' she said tersely, quickly taking her top and skirt off.

'Sorry,' I said.

'What are you pissing apologising for?!'

It was cold and I wasn't so keen on taking my clothes off now, the goose pimples were upon me. I could hardly see so I sat on the single bed to take my shoes off, trying to make out the surroundings. Dirty insipid amber light seeped in to the small room through ragged curtains. There was nothing to look at: no furniture other than the bed and the table, nothing on the walls, no pictures, no wallpaper even. There **was** a dark slash stain, above the head of the bed. I didn't know what it was and I didn't want to know what it was. She'd laid down as I finally took my jeans and boxers off. The message on my boxers was *Get a Grip on Yourself*; I should've listened to my grimeys. In the gloom I could just about make out her body, her dark nipples and pubic hair. It was sufficient.

'Put this on.' She handed me a condom. I was hoping at least she'd put it on for me but it struck me even that would have cost me more. I climbed on top of her, trying to avoid kneeing or kicking her with my awkward legs. Not that she would have felt much pain, she had legs like a Sunday morning rugby league player. And the face of a prop forward, after a long season. Her nipples were pleasingly hard and excited though, but then a gruff *'No feeling, you pay more for that shit!'* tempered my tampering. And then I kissed her, just like in the Beach Boys song. I kissed **her**, she didn't kiss back.

I don't know where but she takes me there... Not really.

'No kissing!' she hissed.

This wasn't love, it wasn't attraction and it wasn't even one of those sordid one night stands, it was a cuttingly cold business transaction. She'd have benefited from a few lessons in Customer Care, I should have told her. With a sudden surge of anger I did my hardest to ram myself into her. Pleasure or pain, I wasn't concerned what sensation she felt, if any. She did gasp for a split second but it was obvious she'd had plenty more visitors before me, and no doubt bigger and heavier. Sensing her lack of anything - it was like riding a slab of barely warm meat - I spent myself quickly. Not that I was ever Valentino before. I climbed off her, feeling used and a user: dirty, sullied, exploited. It wasn't just a feeling, I **was** dirty, sullied, exploited. It was all disgusting; she was disgusting, and as I discarded the filthy condom to the floorboards, I felt the most disgusting of all.

* * *

'Your ma rang earlier, Stevie Redpee,' Dibble said, as I sat down in front of the telly with a plate of Fray Bentos's finest pie and chips on my lap one early evening. If I ever went on to run my own business properly or make my own product, I'd want it to be as good as Fray Bentos Steak & Kidney pies. I loved those pies so much. Talking of business: we'd unfortunately let Lavish fizzle out and eventually fold. It was a shame but we got bored with it and my

going back to my Mum's pretty much finally sealed its fate.

'Said she'd ring back later,' Dibble added.

'Oh, right - cheers Dibs,' I said. *'Was I out then?'*

He was cooking sausages under the grill, and causing a Guy Fawkes dream up the wall behind the cooker as well as causing cat Sam to be nearly alarmed.

'How should I know? You were probably still in bed you lazy bastard!'

There was no need for any aggression, I'd only asked a civil question. To be fair to him, he might have had a point, I did have a kip after work, I'd crashed out for an hour.

Then the phone rang. *'I bet that's her now,'* I said, the same time as he muttered something like *'That'll be the old bat now.'*

'What did you say?' I demanded.

'I said That'll be your ma now. *Why?'* he said, innocently, nearly.

'That's all you better have said.' He didn't give a toss about who he upset or insulted; I mean, my Mum wasn't even fifty yet.

I walked in to the hallway and picked up the receiver of the payphone, closing the living room door behind me.

I'd only just got through half of *'Hello?'* when my Mum's voice amputated the greeting. *'What's this about you buying new furniture without even asking me, this is my house? Stephen? Well?'*

I really did not have a clue what she was talking about - *'Mum, I really do not have a clue what you're talking about.'* I was always pretty good at speaking my mind to my Mum.

'Well that's not what I heard.'

'Well what **have** *you heard?'* Getting grief for a reason is bad enough, but for no reason... I thought I heard a chuckle from the living room. With my Mum mid-rant I stretched and pushed the door open. Dibble was lying on the sofa, relaxed, watching the box. Sam, on the other *paw* - and now curled up in my chair surprise surprise - glanced up at me with a *'Why are you disturbing me, imbecile?'* look.

'Mum,' I interrupted, *'What money, what deposit? What are you on about? Who's told you,* **what** *exactly have they told you?'*

'I rang you earlier, just to see when you're coming home, when your friend - the one who answered, nice boy he sounded, have I met him? - told me you'd been out looking at a new bed. Beds are expensive you know.'

'*I'm not buying any new bed, mother. Why would I?*'

'*Well why would he lie to me? Answer me that. He said you'd been out leaving a deposit on a bed.*'

'*MOTHER, I swear to you! I haven't been leaving a deposit on any...*'. Then it clicked - not the phone but my slow moving brain's answer to this little puzzle.

I covered the mouthpiece and shouted, '*Dibble, you bastard! You said you wouldn't say owt!*' I had to laugh, especially as now I could hear his infectious laugh from behind one of the sofa cushions.

'*I said nowt to her about you knocking off a prozzie, honest!*' he tried to protest, while Sam looked at me with real disdain for the rest of the night.

17 Creepy, Crawly

Love Song - The Damned.

Once, when I split my head open on a Birmingham City stadium girder, the same day of the terrible Bradford Fire, Benny from Miggy commented that if I didn't have bad luck, I wouldn't have any luck at all. I was playing Three Card Brag on the Fullerton coach home and he was looking over my shoulder at my hand - and at the gaping skull slot and congealed lumps of blood - as I frequently snatched defeat from the jaws of victory. Very not unlike our beloved football team in that respect, (un)funnily enough. My cards were marked it turned out, not illegally but with my blood; it got everywhere. I did win the biggest kitty of the day, about a fiver, so it wasn't all bad.

If I was the unfortunate recipient of bad luck - I didn't object to the view, it's unlucky to argue - then Dibble was soon to be the beneficiary of crueller fortune. Actually, he deserved it (and so did I, come to think of it). He just about begged me for help one night and I forgot all about luck as well as the friction he'd caused. All pretty trivial rubbish when compared to real problems. I wanted to help - help the lad who had been the biggest pain in my neck since Jimmy Adamson and the Leeds United Board and the English FA.

'*Steve?*' he had said quietly to me in the Horse and Trumpet while we were playing (losing to) the fruit machine, '*You've had VD ant yer?*'

He said it not quietly enough for my liking.

'*Say it a bit louder why not, they didn't quite hear yer in t'Town Hall.*'

'*Sorry mate.*' Blooming heck, an apology from Dibble - something was definitely up, and he'd called me 'mate'.

'*What's up?*' I asked.

It was, or it had been (up), that was his prickly problem: '*I think I've caught summat.*'

'*Hold yer plums!*' I laughed, pretending to mean the machine, I

130

couldn't resist it. He wasn't amused so I added *'You wanna avoid a dose like the plague, Dibs'* just to be annoying, see how he liked it. By the grimace on his face, I don't think he did.

'I knew that bird from Madison's was dodgy. I shoulda known sum-mat wasn't right when they actually let me in.'

'Maybe you got an infection from a rusty skip?'

'Piss off! Look you splash, I'm asking yer for help, don't be a dick.'

'Alright Dibs, sorry, I feel nearly honoured that you want me to help anyway.'

'I'm desperate.'

I did say *nearly* honoured. *'Desperate? You're Desperate Dib, that's got a nice ring to it.'*

'Are you gonna help me OR WHAT?'

Of course I would; I told him to calm down, I felt bad for him - I knew only too well what he was going through. I did feel quite good for myself too though, I can't deny. It was me who'd had it away with a prostitute after all, it didn't seem right for it to be Dibble suffering from some nasty sexually transmitted infection off a 'non working girl'.

* * *

In the illness of time, there was nearly always something wrong with me. Noses ran in our family, for one thing; or two, nostrilly speaking. It really was true, right through the ages. It was most definitely true with me; every school day virtually without fail, as soon as my feet touched the bedroom carpet I had an allergic reaction in the form of a nasal waterfall. My allergy appeared to be mornings, it was obvious, and drowning in my own fluids wasn't so improbable, I produced snot on a scale of industrial proportions and it made me sick. Streaming eyes, sweating, rivers of mucus pouring from my angry, infuriating and red nose; and always before noon. The common cold was uncommonly common for me, make no mistake, and I detested it and I detested mornings. But then, as afternoon dawned so to speak, everything would turn rosy, I was fine, practically radiant in blooming health. In the mornings, it got so bad I needed two man size hankies to accommodate the flow, and carrying soaking wet and cold handkerchiefs crammed in to my trousers pockets was far from a pleasant. Eventually, I came up with the idea of wrapping used snotrag number one in to an empty crisp packet or such like when it was *snoturated* so as to avoid embarrassing wet patches in my kegs. Let's face it, it was Uri Geller-doubtful you could get more humiliated than being caught with wet patches about your teenage nether regions. When I was at Middle School I did what the wealthy of olden days used to do with hankies - I stuffed them up my sleeve. Henry VIII did it in his day too, and it inspired him to write *Greensleeves*. Obvious really.

I looked like a right lemon, walking around as a kid with lumpy wrists, but it was better than making my nose sorer by wiping it on my sleeve or nearby curtains, coats or classmates, which is what I would have had to do. Using school toilet roll was totally out of the question seeing as they only ever had that horrible plaggy Izal stuff which prompted piles - even in pre teens - and would have ripped my poor snout to even shreddier shreds. Intelligently, Ian told me that the average human suffered from a <u>maximum</u> of two hundred colds in their lifetime. If that was true, then I was special not average, very special as I had well over that number before I was even sixteen.

In 1977, as the Sex Pistols were upsetting the Queen and her Jubilee-celebrating subjects, things got worse. The dreaded TB jab was blazing its way towards the delicate and generally skinny pale arms of my Middle School year. The jab, inoculation against tuberculosis, was notorious for the pain it caused. Kids in the year above took pleasure in showing us the scars on their shoulders, and describing how painful and bulbous the consequent molehill had been. And that wasn't all: before the actual TB jab each child had to be tested with a 'Heath' jab which was not one needle but a small circle of six of the sodding things. I never did like Ted Heath. It might have been five needles. It was definitely *too many* needles, that's what it was. The elder kids tried to convince us *that* injection was agonising too, but I could usually smell a lie - even with a drippy nose - and I didn't believe them. It was a good job I had no phobia with needles - or blood for that matter - otherwise I would have been in a *right* state of unhealth virtually all the time.

The first injection was in the forearm - and it *didn't* hurt - it was the tester: if you developed a swelling then you either had TB or you'd had it before. With either way, as a result you wouldn't need the TB jab. The vast majority of the population never suffered a reaction, and hardly anyone in Beeston, Leeds did this time around. Except for a lad called Harminder that is. Oh, and except for me (that makes two 'excepts' which I don't think sounds right but what the heck). Up sprouted a rather large, itchy, red spot where the injection had mined. As a result, we were given the same jab again a few days later, just to check if the first reaction had been a freak result. It was weird fun; I felt important and it was all quite entertaining. And thankfully there was no reaction this time from the second jab. At least, that applied to Harminder. For me... well, I was the proud owner of a sore and unsightly nipple on *both* forearms now. Nonetheless, I still wasn't that worried - I didn't feel any poorlier and I was actually enjoying having people worrying about me. Wrong of me I know, but I couldn't help it, I liked the attention (we all do I bet, on the quiet). Anyway, it all seemed to be a new, exciting and painless adventure for me.

Until, that is, I started urinating blood.

It wasn't blood, but I wasn't to bleeding know it at the time, no one warned me. If I hadn't been standing at the urinal the first time the red happened, I would have probably shat myself. The doctors at the Chest Clinic in town near the Tower flicks had given me a course of tablets to take for the TB, without warning me there'd be side effects. For all I knew, standing there in the school bogs weeing flat and warm Tizer against the shiny white wall, I could have been literally leaking my life away. Me and George Best *did* have something in common after all! What else was there, what more would happen to me that they hadn't told me about? Was my blood being slowly replaced by yellow pee, would my unfulfilled nuts drop off or would I have multicoloured and luminous stools?
Multicoloured and luminous stools might be fun actually, in hindsight. I could've given them away as presents or even sold them to science (or Man U, as midfielders).

I sprayed my vermilion into the drains, shaking my little soldier like lads should (*'No matter how much you shake your peg, you'll always get a dribble down your leg'* - Nath Archer's dad). I stood for a few seconds, waiting to see if the loss of blood would have any effect. My imagination started to run riot, dreaming headlines for the Evening Post: **STEVE BOTTOMLEY FOUND DEAD IN TOILET - DROWNED IN OWN URINE. AND IT WAS <u>RED</u>!** or **PEA-BRAINED BOY DEAD - DRAINED OF BLOOD IN PEE-DRAIN OF RED!** It turned out my crimson tide was in fact a standard reaction to the tablets. How it was viewed as a 'standard' reaction when I was the only person going through the trauma puzzled me muchly. And regardless of the worry being over, I was still very not happy about it, I felt like I'd been disrespected. Moreso when a couple of kids in the loo noticed the yellow river (*Yellow River, Yellow River*) in front of them slowly turning in to orange. Not unlike a limited edition of UK Subs' *'CID'* single in fact. They promised solemnly to keep it a secret. Yeah right, and I was Prince Charles. There was no incentive for them to keep to their word, and honour amongst schoolboys is a rare thing. So, soon after (like minutes), I had to put up with a new nickname of *'Red Pee Bottomley'* all round school. Brilliant.

The Leeds Chest Clinic was not a nice place to visit, and I felt especially sorry for my Mum having to take me there. The nurses and doctors were fine - and let's face it, I wasn't badly ill like some of the other poor souls - but the building itself was horrible and either always too warm or too chilly. I couldn't believe my visits there with so many unwell people wheezing, coughing, spitting and choking could help anybody - especially me or my Mum - it felt as if you needed a good wash after. Not unlike visiting Old Trafford or London really. It was fun for me though, as it would be for any lad like me with few concerns on the planet to worry about or scare him.

For each appointment, I had to supply a mucus sample in tiny clear plastic containers they provided. And I had to give blood, too - more fun. Anyway, spitting was always one of my favourite playtime pastimes (game of 'Headers' anyone?) and now, I was being asked to snook up and kwoilch as much nasty stuff from my chest and throat as I could, with an audience awaiting! Each morning of an appointment I had to spit in to the container and tighten the bottle top. That was, I decided, to prevent the hazardous stuff I'd gobbed out from escaping. On those mornings, I'd get up early specially, keen as if preparing for a day trip, to growl, grunt and dig deep down for thick, stringy, green, rubbery, brown - or even red if I was really lucky - lung discharge. The walls of our bathroom and my ribcage reverberated with industry. Absolutely disgusting, yes, but I loved to be disgusting, I was a boy, it was natural.

The tablets effectively made me more ill, they were meant to, like a TB exorcism was taking place. It felt like punishment and it hurt a fair bit, in my chest especially, but instead of me being laid low with a horrible cough and breathing difficulties as I expected, it manifested itself in the form of one stinking mother of a godawful cold throughout the entire summer. I regularly ran out of hankies and it ruined my celebrations of the Jubilee I can tell you. And I'd wanted to tuck in to the various street parties like a good un, I had nothing like a punk attitude then even though I was spitting for England. I could hardly breathe, I could hardly sleep - lying on my back would have drowned me while lying on my side practically meant I needed a bowl to stop the pillow from getting saturated. This cold was the stinkiest, stinkier than the most stinky, believe me. During the day I was seriously like a snail, you could find me by the trail of snot I left behind. I was not a happy Loiner.

* * *

Maybe she was ill or just having a bad day, the Samaritans woman. The Samaritans phone line, what a fantastic service, it did my heart good to know there were volunteers out there to help saps like me, or saps like Dibble to be more precise. He was too scared to ring them so I did it for him. I didn't take the mick, he didn't use telephones at work, not in his line of brick bashing and this would have been a scary call to make, I recalled my own from years before. Samaritans surely were, or one day would be, angels, and rightly so. Except this lady, with a posh, quite husky but at the same time not attractive voice, sounded like she should have been calling for advice for herself about depression. At the end I thanked her for the information and nearly asked her if *she* was alright and if I could help.

Dibs was nearly in tears when he told me about the itching and how infuriating it was for him. It's not the sort of stuff you want to be talking about over a drink though - unless you're trying to go on the wagon - but I was quite proud I was the someone he talked to about it. I didn't really want to hear the gory details but sometimes it's best to let people get things out of their system. At first he'd thought it was his bed being too warm, albeit a highly unlikely event in his Headingley abode. It wasn't that, it was something else, something sickening and obscene that he was being brave just telling me, it was that embarrassing for him. We weren't exactly the best of mates after all and he really was reaching out for help - I'd have been the worst kind of friend if I'd let him stew. Mind, I was briefly tempted as I said, I owed him.

Maybe it was bed bugs I suggested, it had to be *something* doing the biting. Maybe it was Sam even, with fleas. No, they'd have noticed him scratching, even if it would have been a very casual and effortless a scratching. There couldn't have been bedbugs in his room in any case, because, he said, his bed sheets were regularly laundered. That wasn't due to him being hygienic but because he peed the bed so often. In fairness, 'so often' wasn't really true but a young man peeing the bed three or four times in a year was far more 'often' than normal behaviour warranted. I'd never peed my bed, not as an adult anyway. Yes, I'd peed in wardrobes, room corners and even in my drawer (my TOP drawer which I'm sure was a physical impossibility) but never in my bed.

When I'd contracted the dose from that witch, it had only struck me during my sleep that I'd caught a wicked infection. Now Dibble was having the same kind of nightmares the poor lad, waking up in cold sweats half the night, as the possibility he'd caught something hit home. Itching, relentless, checking his pubes got such a regular thing, he was getting neck ache he said. Most of all though was the scratching: he'd started bleeding. You can imagine how grateful I was for the info. And then at last he told me he'd spotted one, apparently about two millimetres long. I was tempted to ask if he was sure he'd not actually been looking at his knob but it wouldn't really have been appropriate.
'Are you sure it wasn't in fact your knob you were looking at?' I was

never any good at resisting temptation. He'd nearly laughed, I nearly choked on my beer in surprise. It was like one of those tiny red insects on garden walls in summer he told me, except this wasn't red, it was sort of yellowy green. It didn't take geniuses to work out he'd been to a place where seafood was in season and that he'd caught crabs.

On my own first ever visit - which I'd solemnly planned as my last, too - to the Dose Department at Leeds General Infirmary, the specific ward had been behind a green door in a huge corridor. There was no fun or music behind that green door (just like Shakin bloody Stevens' records then) though there most certainly had been one shaking Stephen. That corridor, busy like Briggate, provided a decent chance of you preserving your anonymity by sneaking, creeping, *diving* in to the door practically unnoticed. Now though, the Special Clinic had moved premises, to a new annexe behind the main outpatients building. Maybe the old clap clinic had become overrun with lice and stuff, maybe the surgical implements had gotten rusty and maybe the doors were stuck shut by discharge or the locks scabbed over. Maybe I was thinking too much about it all, full stop.

Obviously I wasn't as nervous as Dibble as it wasn't me afflicted but I *was*. I was worried about what people might think, of two lads going together to the 'special' clinic. So I wore a woolly Leeds hat to try and stay undercover. When I'd gone the first time I didn't have a clue what to expect other than the disgusting Umbrella my mates had spoken of. Now, a little bit older and more experienced, I tried to keep Dibble relaxed. I failed miserably, mainly because he kept asking me what they'd do, what vicious implements they'd stick in him and how much pain he'd feel. I couldn't lie to him. Come the day I took a sicky and I met him dead early (half eight always felt dead early for me) hoping for not just his sake that the ordeal would be over quickly. The Pox Docs now operated, so to speak, from a temporary block near one of the many car parks the LGI possessed. To their credit, it was sign-posted pretty well so there was no need to ask complete strangers where we should go to get my friend's knob rot sorted. I'd have asked in a very deep voice if I had asked though, mark my words.

It was a neat building block - like a temporary Portakabin really - with a new cement ramp running up to the door. There were many cars parked around but no people whatsoever. Relief: this would be one smooth entry over with in little time. With a hearty slap on his back in an attempt to boost his confidence I led him up the slope. His eyes hardly left the ground, I could almost feel his shame. I wasn't exactly proud myself but he was really toiling, it was woeful. Lifting my own eyes briefly from the ground as we walked, two young female nurses looked down at us from a window. Not only did that indicate they weren't very busy this morning, the way they smiled cheerfully made me think it all might not be so bad for Dibs after all. God knows, we might even pull! But then I looked across from the window at the building wall. Leering at us was a clear sign we'd gone wrong somewhere, <u>literally</u> a clear sign, printed in blue and white: 'Women's Ward'. Bollocks, the Men's was the next block down. Flushing redder than a baboon's arse we very quickly turned around to flee. Glancing up at the nurses one last time though I saw they were loving our disaster, laughing away. I couldn't stop myself grinning back, like the fool I was. Dibble, eyes stuck to the ground and not seeing the funny side so much - well not at all - spat *'You arsehole, you better not have meant to do that!'*

* * *

Naturally I didn't join him in the inspection but he told me in graphic detail what had gone on. He seemed to have forgotten I'd been in the same situation before and I really wasn't keen to relive any of it. It didn't stop him mind, but I wouldn't want to repeat the horrible details. I mean, having the crabs was humiliating enough for him to have to reveal to the doctor - the *female* doctor at that - but at least she sorted it out swiftly. He didn't even have to go on any tablets so it meant he could go on the beer straight away. I'd had it much worse that time. Not that I was looking for a medal or anything. For me to go through the intricacies of the Umbrella being wedged in to his sausage *too far* and to describe the subsequent tiny javelin trauma inflicted on his todger wouldn't be right. No one would want to hear about it unless they were looking to rip him to shreds with sarcasm. So we kept the whole sorry and sore tale private. I had one hell of a story over him now, he'd be mad to wind me up too much.

I did though feel genuinely uplifted about myself for helping a friend out, it made me glow knowing I'd done some good.

It took only a few days for his unwanted population to be killed off. I was half surprised Dibble didn't have students campaigning outside the house with a *'Pubic Lice Have Rights Too'* placards. Well maybe not. He bought me a few beers as a thank you, I bought him some back to say it was no trouble, I was proud to have helped and to have gained a better friendship out of it.

18   This Grace Under Pressure

On Saturday the 21st of February 1987, nearly thirty-two thousand of us saw the rebirth of Leeds United. And it was beautiful! Billy's Boys had trundled along in Division Two all season, earning some decent results along the way but then totally spoiling the progress with rubbish defeats or draws. Somehow though, on the quiet, they'd managed to get to the 5th Round of the FA Cup too, and First Division QPR had been pulled out of the hat to visit Elland Road. We were possibly just three wins away from Wembley.

It wasn't just a surprise to the fans that we'd progressed so far in the Cup, it was clearly a bit of an eye-opener for the Leeds officials on the day of the game as well. They had to lock hundreds of supporters out as so many turned up late to pay at the turnstiles. Consequently, people climbed trees, lampposts, vehicles, each other, straining to see in to the stadium as the match started, while scores congregated on the overlooking quarry or even from the roof of the Peacock pub. I was one of the lucky many to get in but only just, it was 2.20pm when I made it in to the ground, forty minutes before kick off but only five before they started turning people away in their droves, for safety reasons. And what a match it was too.

Finely balanced at 1-1, late on we got a corner at my/the Kop end. I seem to remember Micky Adams floated a cross over to the near post, Big John Pearson flicked it on and a perfectly timed run from lionhearted defender Brendan Ormsby won it with a bazooka of a header which stretched the white net. 2-1 to Leeds and now we were virtually only two wins away from the Wembley Twin Towers! Everyone went mental, including the players clambering on to the railings to celebrate as close as possible with the ecstatic Koppites. Leeds United, so often garbage in the cup competitions were, as a lowly Second Division club, suddenly in the last eight - the Quarter Finals of the most famous club competition in the world, the FA Cup.

As a direct result of this adventure, Leeds' League form picked up dramatically too and I for one finally knew, I just **knew,** the cup run would prove crucial for our promotion push. We were definitely heading for long awaited promotion, returning to the top division where we belonged; I was almost clairvoyant in the knowledge. Admittedly, we might have to do it via the play-offs but do it we would, doubtless was I, doubtless. And we might even get to Wembley for the Cup Final too, put that in your hype and smoke it! Having said that, I had a sneaking suspicion that Coventry City had their name already engraved on the trophy, they were great underdogs and playing really well. Whatever, this was still all massive, unbelievable fun and I had to be calmed down in the pub many a time whilst babbling on about the absolute true faith in my head.

Football fans' notoriety was rife, like a stench of rotting and sour across the world, and we Leeds fans were just about the worst of the lot, apparently, allegedly. Many folk loved to hate us, especially the media who put the wind up the rest of the nation with stories and myths of the *evil* that masqueraded as followers of everyone's favourite targets, 'dirty' Leeds. The Stranglers strangely enough, had to put up with a similar reputation in the music business too. Obviously it seemed there was no justice. Leeds fans had to put up with bans, decimated away game ticket allocations and ridiculous kick off times for matches, Sunday mornings for instance. It made me laugh too, when every single pub in the relevant area was forced to close to prevent fans drinking before a game. It never stopped George Best and certain other players before they played so why should it stop us supporters? All you needed to do was drink right through the night before or get canned up prior to the match, nice and chilled in the fridge, and cheaper than the pubs'. Simple. Too much trouble though did go on, it couldn't be denied. Too much was made of it as well mind, and that was the truth. Certainly more than enough people in authority who didn't know what they were talking about were doing the talking, and the banning. I'd been present at lots of football incidents and some would see that as my being guilty. But what could I do about it, really? I wasn't going to jack my team in just because of people's mistaken suspicions. There was no doubt the violence had become more and more sickening, especially when people, usually innocents, got badly injured or even killed at football matches across Europe.

* * *

Leeds were drawn away at Wigan Athletic in the FA Cup Quarter Final. I predicted we'd win, I knew we would, to be honest; cocky though I was being. Wigan fought gamely enough but even on a horrible pitch and windy conditions, we came out comfortable winners. John Stiles (son of the great Nobby and thankfully better looking) and the nearly always impressive Micky Adams scored our goals with Wigan coming close only a couple of times. Courtesy of the Fullerton I was one of the relatively few Leeds fans there and it was a good day out, even though, predictably, we had to miss pre-match bevvying in the process of that Sunday game.

Although we didn't all go to Leeds games, each and every one of my Beeston and Headingley mates and the Cross Flatts team were devout Leeds fans, and Leeds' performances in the latter half of the '86/'87 season inspired and thrilled us all. We had more and more players wanting to play for the Flatts and there were regularly at least a dozen of us out on a Friday and Saturday night. And - this is the truth - though we *heard* of trouble in Leeds involving gangs of Leeds fans, doormen and the police, I never saw one sniff, not one sniff, of violence in town. There was never any doubt my lot could look after themselves but the need was never called for, fortunately. The closest I came to a fight was in the Tommy Wass: some halfwit with curly hair cheered when Argentina scored against England. He was asking for it but I'd have had to join the queue to lamp him. He made his hasty excuses and left, hastily.

* * *

There were over fifty thousand Leeds and Coventry fans at the Semi Final. Even though they had less fans than us, Coventry were given more than half the available tickets by the FA. They didn't even sell their entire quota. The FA and the police were terrified that the heathen hooligan element of Leeds fans would cause carnage and chaos in Sheffield that Sunday lunchtime. I've never seen as many police on duty as that day, it was like a national gathering of Bobbies. Walking down to the Hillsborough stadium was like being part of a huge ocean of human beings, and all Leeds human beings. Sensational, and all in good spirits, in party mood, for this our biggest game for years. Even though loads of fans were late - with dozens of cars and coaches just abandoned on roadsides and verges - I didn't witness any trouble. The club, management and players had all stated over the previous few weeks their hopes the fans would behave well and make it a good day to remember for us all. It all whiffed of responsible lip service but you couldn't blame them and after all, it was the right thing to do. I'd managed to get a ticket with Mike in the seats at the side of the pitch opposite the tunnel. At the far end there were gaps in the terraces where Coventry supporters were, whereas to my right, the Leppings Lane End terraces were absolutely, well and truly - unbelievably - crammed with Leeds fans. It was a scorching day, too, I was glad I was in the shade.

The game was a classic, the neutrals said that and even the anti Leeds media said it. And how both teams performed gained them much admiration and loads of new fans. It will go down in Leeds United legend how well we played, the goals we scored and the goals we gave away. My heart weighed heavy for our players who made crucial mistakes that day and that's why I've never named/blamed them since. They'd been all vital in getting us so far in the FA Cup anyway. Leeds United at that time had some fantastically spirited players who, if not the most skilful had such grit and determination they would never dream of giving anything but their all for the white shirt, just like the faithful who stuck by them in the dark seasons.

As I said many a time, there was no way Leeds would not achieve promotion after such a magnificent display, no way, the proverbial writing was on the football wall; it was high excitement. Both sets of fans had a great day out, backing their teams passionately and deafeningly throughout. The two teams were avidly applauded off the field by all the fans. We lost 3-2 (after extra time) and the Coventry players did a lap of honour around the whole pitch. To people not actually at the game, doing such a thing was a bad idea just asking for trouble from the waiting/wanting-to-be-incited Leeds hordes. This would be the moment Leeds fans would sour a great occasion (yet again) in scenes of riot and violence, with all the nation - and, more importantly, the media - eagerly awaiting. Except, of course, the only things thrown by Leeds fans at the Coventry players was plaudits, cheers and congratulations. That's what football was really about. I was well pleased with how our team had played that day but I tell you what, I was happier still with the fans. We'd been through so much together and this was one more occasion of sorrow we had to endure, but we did it, with grace and dignity. Mike put his arm around me as I swallowed the tears - tears of dejection in defeat but also tears of pride at the unity and decency of Leeds fans.

* * *

Whether I deserved it or not, loneliness was so often a heavy pain. It might have been the consequences of the alcohol or just my bad judgement to blame. Whichever, it wasn't that important, all I need to say is that solitude hurt me badly. I often allowed myself to wallow in self-pity, and it was shameful of me I know it. Such times though eventually taught me how important family and friends are, to keep you appreciated, to keep you in reality. *And* to keep you mentally healthy. When you're down, you should call on them to help lift you. No one is ever truly alone, despite what it can feel like, and it's not *using* people, it's sharing. When a person helps another person, *they* feel good too, it's mutual benefit and it's human nature.

So who needed a girlfriend when I had this feeling of communal spirit and belonging? And who needed the 'security' of a safe, humdrum and uninspiring career? Who needed to drink their self stupid just for the sake of it? Not me mate, at least not anymore. It had taken some years but I realised that beer was not such a good friend after all, it screwed my head up well and truly. Anyway, I had great family and friends plus a football team to be proud of again. With thousands of brothers and sisters, I had the resurrection of Leeds United to help me along. Proud as peacocks, march on together to good times, that's what we'd do, and very soon.

* * *

There are times when you surprise yourself. Sometimes pleasantly, sometimes not. This particular evening was one of those positive times - all the more surprising as it happened to be one of the worst nights of my life as well. Our coach was crawling home from Birmingham along with scores of others and the mood on board was darker than the night sky.

Defeat in football, in big games, happens all the time. Obviously. And often it's predictable too, right from the very kick off. Your team hasn't 'turned up' and they just aren't 'at the races'. In other words, in plain English, they're not good enough on the day and deserve to lose to a better team, frustrating and unappetising as that is for all concerned. We'd seen it happen too many times with Leeds, their fortunes were like a Shakespeare tragedy waiting to happen.

But not tonight, no way: it's the 1987 Division 2 Play Off Final Replay, between Leeds United and Charlton Athletic. The winner wins promotion to the top division.

Leeds have been excellent throughout and the better team.
The players have run their selves into the ground for the white cause, in what has been an extremely long and debilitating season. Poor old centre-half Ormsby, a real Leeds battler and leader, has badly injured his knee in the match. And then to add near-exhaustion to the depleted team, the match goes to extra time. The tension's killing me, killing us all. I'm so nervous my guts are having a field day. Leeds get a free kick just outside the Charlton penalty area. John Sheridan, young midfield maestro and excellent dead-ball striker, prepares to take it. He bends to plant the ball down. He straightens up, standing tall, authoritative, in control. He's pointing, directing, gesticulating at his team-mates, positioning them around the opponents' goal. He steps back, still pointing, still directing, and he pauses. He's not satisfied with the players and he continues to tell them. Stepping forward now, still pointing, still directing, still signalling. *And still pretending.* Suddenly he strikes the ball. It flies cleanly over the defensive wall. It takes the defence by sur-

prise and the ball speeds towards goal. The Charlton 'keeper is practically stunned, seeing the ball dart past him and crash into the net. It's 1-0 to Leeds, in their most important game for years, and there's only a few minutes to go.

We erupt in celebration, thousands of us. Arms reaching and punching the sky, all around me. It's chaos, beautiful, joyous chaos. I don't think I've ever seen it as mad before, not even in the Coventry game. Here is passion and ecstasy, *football* passion and ecstasy, it's unparalleled, and I'm well and truly a part of it, immersed in the ocean of yellow, white and blue. I'm dancing with Mike, I'm hugging him, I'm hugging guys I've never met before, I smell the beer on their breath and the aromas of hygiene and anxiety on them, and the release of tension. We tumble, we bump, we fall, we help each other get up and then we topple over again. I'm nearly in tears and I'm losing my voice. I'm not actually saying anything, I'm just roaring, stretching my vocal cords in celebration. I can almost feel the buzz of the away days to come, of Anfield, Old Trafford, Highbury, White Hart Lane and the rest. I'm losing my mind with delirium, my head and heart rise like a thermometer, close to bursting the scale with pride. Then I *am* in tears, as I sense my Dad is here rejoicing with me, and I sense he's happy knowing that Mike looks after me, like an uncle.

Minutes later, near the end of the match, we've calmed down and my insides feel like they've plummeted in tragedy: Charlton have equalized, and with a weak goal - poor marking and defending. Had Ormsby still been on the pitch Charlton would not have got through, simple fact. But they have and Mervyn Day could only look in bewilderment at the ball nestled in his net. Jesus, it always has to be a roller coaster ride with Leeds, so many ups and downs it's unbelievable. Typical though too, and we will forgive them just like we always have before. It simply means we'll have to win by penalties, that's all, and with the recent big-game experience in their armoury the Leeds players will be ready for it. I think I'd only seen a game go to penalties once before, against Liverpool at Wembley in the Charity Shield. Leeds lost then but this time they will be prepared, Billy will have made plans for it, he will have left nothing to chance. Then Charlton get another corner.

The whole scene is just like before, the players' positions, the areas of danger, the referee's placement even. And shite, it's on the cruel cards, Charlton score again, with a virtually identical and hideously soft goal yet again. Leeds are done for now, no way can the players recover, it's been a horrendously tough season and it's Game Over, we are well and truly done for.

* * *

Those Leeds players, gallant in such brave defeat and undoubtedly exhausted, had exhausted us all too. My seeing grown men in the crowd, as well as many of the players distraught and in tears, caused me to bloody well sob long after the final whistle had gone. The small number of Charlton fans dancing on their terrace made it even worse.

Me, supremely confident we'd win promotion; me, *clairvoyant*? My overfull backside, what a prick, I needed a good talking to. I was disgusted with myself, ashamed at my arrogance. Something soon told me though, that if I was to recover and not over-traumatise about it all, I needed to lift myself and be positive, quickly. This obviously would be no easy task, given the funereal atmosphere on the packed coach after the game. It would be the moment and the platform of my surprising myself.

You know the sort of person who always tries to look on the bright side of life, no matter how grim a situation or how annoying they're being? There could be an incurable epidemic or a horrible genocide, and this individual will pipe up with *'Worse things happen at sea'* or *'What will be will be, it's fate'* and all that. What a right royal pain in the Whitehall Farce they are. Their glass is always half-full, not half-empty, and they think they're being brave and helpful by being so sodding cheerful and optimistic. Sometimes there are *no* positives to consider and those are the occasions when people like that deserve a good slap, to bring them to their senses and to stop spoiling normal people's lives. EXCEPT, there's me, on the Fullerton coach, still in shock at the most bitter defeat since Paris 1975, and a dazzling idea strikes me: the 'troops' need rallying, as do I. The Leeds United march must not falter because of the defeat, and I can play a big part in our recovery.

So *'Let's play that Alphabet game,'* I announce.

There were a few grumbles and chunters, and even Mike gave me a sharp nudge, but no one actually replied or gave me a thump. I tried again. *'COME ON, LADS! Let's have a game of Alphabet, like Parts of the Body or summat. We need to have a laugh.'*

'Shut up, you tit, no one's in t'mood for chuffing games,' shouted a pained voice from the backseat.

'Hear hear,' agreed someone nearer.

I wasn't beaten; in fact I was more motivated, more intent on trying to lift the mood. *'Don't you two play then,'* I hoped not to sound aggressive as I said it. *'Come on, we can't afford to get depressed over the result, we'll be back.'*

'Steve, I think you've got it wrong this time, mate,' said Banksy in a soft tone. I always liked Banksy, he was fun but mature and respected. *'There's loads on this coach who've seen loads more games than you'*, he said, *'and this result tonight, is possibly the worst ever. I can't see the club coming back from it.'*

'You might be right, Banksy,' I said, *'but with that attitude we might as well all pack it in. And what would be the point of that? It's not the Leeds way and it's not what being Leeds supporters is about. As far as I know, it never has been either. It's about never giving in, always supporting the team and... well, supporting each other.'*

'You're just a kid, you don't know what you're talking about,' came the voice from the backseat again.

'I'm twenty-one, I'm not that young, And I'm only trying to cheer us up! I'm just as gutted as you lot y'know, we're all in the same boat.'

'Bollocks!' he shouted.

'To you an' all! It's like the song - We've been through it all together, and we've had our...'

'No, I said bollocks,' came the backseat bigmouth again. *'Let's play your stupid bloody game then, Parts of the Body, and I start, B - for Bollocks.'*

I laughed. *'What about starting with A like normal people?'*

'Who's normal on here?'

'Arsehole then!' someone else remarked, I hoped it was a contribution to the game and not an insult for me. More obscene words followed, in alphabetical order, or *dis*order I should say, as the number of players grew as we progressed.

It's all straightforward, it's all obvious: it's not Game Over at all and it never can be. No, it has a rest and then it starts all over again.

* * * *

Thanks and other stuff

None of this would have been produced without Ian Daley of Route's influence. He gave me a chance years ago and I grabbed it, with *One Northern Soul.* You might be interested to know why *No More Heroes* isn't on Route, too. If you are, well I'll tell you. If you're not, skip the next paragraph. Be like that then, see if I care.

At the risk of being seen as egotistical, arrogant or even greedy, there are simple reasons for this being a Relish Books title. I decided Relish should publish it because I wanted it out earlier and this seemed quite easily the quickest way. More importantly, I wanted to receive more of the profits - please Lord, let there be some, hey hey - to enable Relish to invest in more new works by new writers: that's what I set out to do in the first place with Relish Books.

And of course there are other people who have been even greater help in making *NMH* possible, not least *you* as you read this, having bought (*bought* and not borrowed from a mate!) the book. Chris Archer, in creating the cover, has been top support, and then there's those guys who have been very helpful, integral even, in certain tales within the book. Adam Grimshaw and Martin McGowan, take a bow, for dramatised events which do NOT involve the more 'adult' moments in the story, before dubious connections are made. Plus Andy Bartle, Mr & Mrs Brewer, Mr & Mrs Ellis, Dave & Darren Brydon, Richard L. Gomersall, David B. Rowbotham and obviously Everton Campbell and Peter G. 'Bruges' Robinson, all kind of appearing in the story. And you, Mark Campbell, I still can't believe I wasn't one of your regular first choices for the Flatts. I constantly look hard and long in search of forgiveness for you, but it just isn't anywhere to be found in my scarred and affected soul. Shame on you!

Then there's Jackie Beedle and Jane Selby, two women who volunteered to read and appraise early drafts and who weren't at all shy in their constructive criticisms and suggestions. Their editing support has been great and much appreciated. Not forgetting of course the friends who have stuck by me in my 'career' for seemingly ever, some of whom I haven't seen for ages (I'll take the blame for that) and some of whom have put their money where their mouths are, so to speak. Massive thanks for that is permanent. And of course, my family - two families I suppose, the Endeacotts and the Bruces - in which exist probably my biggest critics even when they're unaware of it. The criticism is always said and received in the right context, honest, I stopped blubbing about it years ago. Well, months anyway. You won't find many better than my Bruce family, I'll tell you that for nowt, kidder. There's also the Euro Polymers 'family' in Leeds, led by Steve the main-man Horn, along with Jaimes, Jason and even red Steve Shaw, all who've been great help for me and for Relish.

Plus Tom Palmer, Gary Kaye, Gary Edwards, Deborah, Rachel (times two) and Xav.

I sincerely hope you have enjoyed this book and want to read more. Or *write* more even. As you read this - well done for keeping your eyes open in such adversity! - I'm working on my next novel. Well, more than one actually: the thing is, I haven't completely decided on which one yet, so please look out for news on the Relish website. At the moment, 'Hang the DJ' is prominent in my head, but so is 'All You Need Is Luv' and a new idea called 'April Fools'.
And then there's 'The World Famous Standards' too, which should be fun plus some great books by 'new' Relish writers.

Robert Endeacott, March 2005

RELISHING IT!

It's Relish Books' aim to publish original and entertaining works. 'Humbugs' was our first title, 'Fanthology' our second and 'No More Heroes' the third (fourth after a lovely, unofficial little 'Bump' actually). We want to give people who might not have had opportunity before, chance of being published. There is no great strategy or secret - if it's original and good, we want to read it and ensure it gets a fair chance.

Relish Books will never be a huge company - that may or may not be a good thing, I'm not quite sure - but we're in it for the right reasons: the Writers and Readers, the most important people in literature. Relish Books will sink if we don't listen, so please do get in touch, we need you.

Ideas, contacts, thoughts, criticisms, support, help... you name it, we'll listen.

And you might think you can do better than the titles so far. Well, please let us know, we might take you up on them. And of course we might not, but we will certainly consider all correspondence and reply to them.

*Check out the Relish website **www.relishbooks.co.uk*** for more details - no unsolicited material though please, it's not fair on us or the good postmen of Leeds!

email robert@relishbooks.co.uk

Humbugs

Craig Bradley & David Gill
(Relish Books, ISBN 0-9547844-0-5)

When life gets a bit empty, you need something to fill the hole. For the lads and lasses of the toffee-making factory works team, football provides the filling.

'Humbugs', a story of toffee-making folk not giving a toffee about making toffee. A story of toffee-making folk who do give a toffee about their workmates and teammates. And who seriously give a toffee about taking the mick.

A tasty pick 'n' mix of chuntering, chuckling, cheating, cheap bribery, cheap *jibery*, cheap trickery and downright cheap challenges.

Humbugs, because not everything in life is black and white.

'Punchily written, earthy and pulsing with the rhythms of Halifax vernacular - a truly funny read.' The Halifax Courier.

'... a refreshing read, unassuming and delightfully unglamorous.' The Leeds Guide.

'I laughed so much my au pair had to help me up after I'd fallen off my pearl-crusted commode!' an England football spokesman.

AVAILABLE FROM GOOD BOOKSHOPS and
www.relishbooks.co.uk.

One Northern Soul

J R Endeacott
(Route, ISBN 1-901927-17-2)

Tales of grim humour and charm from the early 80's of a Leeds boy growing up without a father, a job or even a half-decent football team to follow. But this is a boy, and a team, with hope available if it's looked for in the right places.

Unfortunately, it never seems to be.

Pretty stories alongside pretty ugly ones, this is essential reading. The 'predecessor' to 'No More Heroes'.

'A poignant and at times laugh out loud snapshot of the adolescent years of one Stephen Bottomley. CHAMPION.' Big Issue In The North.

'... anyone who bought their Stranglers records from the excruciatingly named Scene & Heard, or drank next door in the Precinct (possibly the hardest pub in Leeds) will want to read this book. And those who have not, should.' The Yorkshire Post.

'Great read, good laugh, very poignant.' Damon Timm, USA.

'A must for football fans everywhere.' Icky, Beeston.

AVAILABLE FROM GOOD BOOKSHOPS or www.route-online.com or directly from the author (see www.relishbooks.co.uk).

Fanthology

Robert Endeacott & Graeme Garvey
(Relish Books, ISBN 0-9547844-0-5)

Many descriptions of Leeds United have been thrown at Leeds United AFC... never can the words 'boring' or 'mundane' be used.

Throughout the frequent highs and frequent lows of this world famous team, the fans have been there every step and tumble of the way. 'Fanthology' lets them - over fifty of them, including celebrities - do the talking, with superb stories and anecdotes to entertain not just football fans but readers in general.

There are famous Leeds fans within Fanthology, standing on the terraces of literature alongside less well known ones, from all over the world. Each has a touching story to tell in this a real treat for all.

'... what a classic it is... There's something to appeal to everyone... it's all here.' Yorkshire Evening Post, Nov. 2004.

'... this brilliant book... comprises over 200 pages stuffed with passion, hopes, dreams and memories. Buy it for a Leeds fan you know, now. Then buy one for someone who supports some other club - and make them jealous.'
Leeds Leeds Leeds magazine, Jan. 2005.

'A must read for all football fans.' Lynn, UK.

'... this was not the kind of book I normally thought I would like so much, but as soon as I started reading it, I found it difficult to put down.' Amazon - 'a reader', Leeds.

AVAILABLE FROM GOOD BOOKSHOPS or directly from
www.relishbooks.co.uk

Paint It White - Following Leeds Everywhere

Gary Edwards
(Mainstream, ISBN 1-84018-729-8)

'Paint It White' is Gary Edwards' unique and hilarious account of the scrapes, adventures and times of comedy that a life's passion for Leeds United has brought him.

'Excellent read!!! Gary's book brought the memories flooding back! I could recall many of his experiences, from the heights of the European trips in the 70's to the lows of the early 80's.' J A Lyons, Dewsbury.

'Even more essential reading for Leeds fans! Gary Edwards nearly chinned me in the Kop in 1979 but regardless, Paint It White is a belting read. If you're a Leeds fan you'll find it hard to put this book down. If you're not, from this book you can at last find genuine explanation as to football fanaticism while enjoying many a chuckle along the way! Gary's a Number 1 fan and this book is a Number 1 read.'
Relish Books review, 2004.

AVAILABLE FROM GOOD BOOKSHOPS

And coming soon, Gary's eagerly anticipated follow up, the 'Second Coat'!

If You're Proud to be a Leeds Fan

Tom Palmer
(Mainstream ISBN 1840185740)

Leeds United Football Club have one of the worst reputations in the country: a history of players, fans and managers that supporters of other clubs love to accuse.

Tom Palmer tries to work out if that is true. The book examines the highs and lows of the club's recent history - from the Paris riots in 1975 to relegation in 1982 and the glory of the 1992 League win.

Written in 2002, it's a reminder of what things will be like when Leeds United are back where they belong.

'A good read. Palmer tackles deep and difficult issues with plenty of angst, in a blunt, forthright, yet humorous manner.' Four Four Two

'Palmer's book is far better than previous supporters' offerings and is a must for United fans.' Yorkshire Evening Post

AVAILABLE FROM GOOD BOOKSHOPS

All This Is Mine

Ray French
(Vintage ISBN 0-099-45533-1)

South Wales, 1968, and ten year old Liam is grappling with some big questions. Is he adopted? Is it true he'll live to be a 108 if he drinks a glass of his own pee every day? Why does everyone laugh at his dad behind his back? The more he sees of the adult world, the less he understands. Until he makes friends with Marek.

I would die for Poland. Would you die for Wales?

Marek, the son of Polish immigrants, reveals that the Russians are planning to stage a coup and take over Wales, just like they did in Poland. Liam and Marek form the resistance and begin a desperate campaign of sabotage. Meanwhile, at home, Liam finds no matter how hard he tries, he just can't make his parents love each other. And what are the strange noises coming from the cellar in the middle of the night?

'One of the very few writers who can remember precisely what childhood was really like, how crazy and intense it really was. Utterly unpretentious, totally engaging and very funny' - Mark Haddon, author of The Curious Incident Of The Dog In The Night-Time.

'Ray French has written a highly engaging and vivid debut novel, which perfectly captures the wild emotions of boyhood... It is a richly satisfying piece of storytelling' - The Daily Telegraph.

'French's hilarious dialogue brings the world of this late 60s community to life, as with a sure hand he sketches in poignant views of the joys, sadness and sheer ghastliness of childhood (and children)' - The Guardian.

AVAILABLE FROM GOOD BOOK SHOPS